MW00876202

Santa Barbara Literary Journal

Volume 8: *Moon Drunk*

December 2022

Editors

Silver Webb, Editrix

Shelly Lowenkopf, Poetry Editor

Dennis Russell, Music Man

Maryanne Knight, Assistant Editor

Santa Barbara Literary Journal
Santa Barbara, CA, U.S.A.
www.santabarbaraliteraryjournal.com

Published by Borda Books

ISBN: 9798362988586

"When you're writing, you're conjuring. It's a ritual, and you need to be brave and respectful and sometimes get out of the way of whatever it is that you're inviting into the room."

—Tom Waits

Table of Contents

5

Lyrics

6

Down the Rabbit Hole

Art

Dear Reader,

And so, we arrive at 8. Four years in, and Lit Jo remains a beacon of dignity. Ha! But there is something to be said for longevity, for refusing to fold under the vagaries of life. To remain creative, even when it's not convenient, profitable, or even pleasant. In fact, my most revered writers, musicians, and artists are those who have endured over the course of a lifetime, and continue to create, regardless of where the spotlight wanders. Bob Dylan is still touring for fantastic new songs. Patti Smith still blows my mind. David Bowie recorded and released *Blackstar* at 69, a few months before he left this dimension. It comes down to this: musicians *must* play, artists *must* paint, and writers *must* write. Anything less that this imperative, and you end up the forgotten member of a boy band, or designing bologna labels, or calling it quits after you self-publish your memoir (Oh, yes, I just said that. Quote me on it.)

Lit Jo occasionally tips its hat to these enduring artists, and Volume 8 continues the tradition. Tom Waits is prolifically creative, and has been since his twenties, as a musician and actor. The gravelly voice, the wildly unpredictable, profane and whimsical lyrics accompany a love affair with the piano that borders on infidelity to his wife. He is the kind of musician who has been playing for long enough that you remember whole decades of your life based off a particular album of his. The really good artists do this; they walk with you through your life. His song, "Drunk on the Moon," was released two years after I was born, on *The Heart of Saturday Night*. The lyrics had me at "And the moon's a silver slipper / It's pouring champagne stars / Broadway's like a serpent / Pulling shiny top-down cars." Volume 8 is thus titled "Moon Drunk," in honor of the song and the singer, and also because there is a dreamlike, blurred quality to his music and the moon itself that also describes a kind of story I love to read. I hope you will enjoy looking for both the moon and the surreal in this volume, which begins with James-Paul Brown's beautiful artwork on the cover, and winds through a path of poetry, curated by Shelly Lowenkopf (look for "It is Late and Dark and You're No Lantern" by Amy McNamara), flash ("And She Lay There in the Moonlight" by Ted Chiles and "Blue Hour" by Chella Courington are favorites), and into short stories like "Destination Unknown" by Max Talley. Be sure to check out our Lyrics section, curated by Dennis Russell, as well as the world-famous "Down the Rabbit Hole" with DJ Palladino, featuring excerpts from his novel, *Werewolf, Texas*.

Many thanks go to my family, the fabulous editing crew at Lit Jo, and the circle of writers and artists in Santa Barbara that make this such a wonderful place to live and write.

Best,
Silver Webb
The Editrix

LISTENING TO THE MOON

by Heather Bartos

When all was said and done, there wasn't anything left to say or do. She packed up all the bits and pieces, all the pauses between words, the sentence fragments and run-ons, and walked away. I couldn't stop wondering why. She couldn't stop to wonder.

"I don't see how," she said weeks earlier, between smooth, bleached teeth, "how it is that you can work with clients, all day long, and say you do nothing."

"Well, because I do."

"You listen to them, don't you?" she asked. "Don't they have things they want to accomplish?"

Accomplishment is our family's sacred purpose. Our daughter is a lawyer. Our son is studying medicine. Our other son, afraid of his potential at the peak of the bell curve, sits enthroned in a recliner watching Sponge Bob. He stays inside, fearful of sunburn.

If I asked my wife to look at a sunset, she'd say, "That's nice. But what does it do?" It's easier for her to understand the sun. The sun allows plants and people to grow and consume. It encourages suburban parents to jog around and around, chasing kids and careers, going nowhere, preserving those stainless-steel arteries for more pointless pursuit. It shines its approval down upon them as they run.

But a sunset? A reflection, rather than the real thing. What does it do? What does it produce?

I listen for the moon. Everyone sees the sun. It's the big, bright distraction, the fears and dreams that generate the weather of our lives. It wakes you up. When it goes away, so do you, into darkness and sleep.

The moon comes out only when the sun is gone. It's a parasite, sucking and sapping light, but it has a peculiar power and pull all its own. It holds the reasons we don't give for the things we shouldn't do, the excuses we would give if we knew what needed apology. It pushes the oceans to nibble the strongest, most sturdy sandcastles into grains of sand.

The word "lunacy" comes from the Latin word for "moonstruck"—*lunaticus*.

You are incomplete until you listen to the moon.

I go into the living room, where little living is being done. My son stares at the TV. His "vacancy" sign is on.

I listen for the moon. I push the couch away from the wall and empty a bookcase. Then I pull it away too.

"What are you doing?" he asks.

"Listening," I say. I drag the lamp and end table away. I go into the garage, into what was supposed to be my tool area. I never liked Home Depot. I never saw anything I could fix.

Here they are.

I open my oil paints, my pastels, the colors of jewels, of irises and hummingbirds, the glamor and glow of sunsets over turquoise waves.

Here you are.

"What are you doing?" my son repeats.

"What are you doing?" I ask.

I brush off the wall with my palm, a blessing, and then I begin.

IT IS LATE AND DARK AND YOU'RE NO LANTERN

by Amy McNamara

is it your ghost there drawing
my eye

to the edge
of the canvas?

your thumb smudge
in the corner

caught in one of those poison
oil pigments, Paris

green—white spirits
couldn't take it off   .

maybe you stopped working
to listen to wind in the alley

or take a bite
of a forgotten sandwich
and there you left

your small print whorl

it is always this way between us
the gauzy curtain

of your vanishing point
and my wide-faced blinking

when I sleep
and my hair is damp, frantic,

plastered to my forehead,
I believe it is your thumb
pulling me up, away from my tangle

don't you roll
that earnest plank toward me
and call it bed,

cow eyes, I want the devil
in my cherry
orchard

trammeling innocent petals
in contrast
to their begetting

raven-headed hair puller
scamper up a branch
or two & we'll

sweeten & shiver down
some blooms
of our own

GAME.

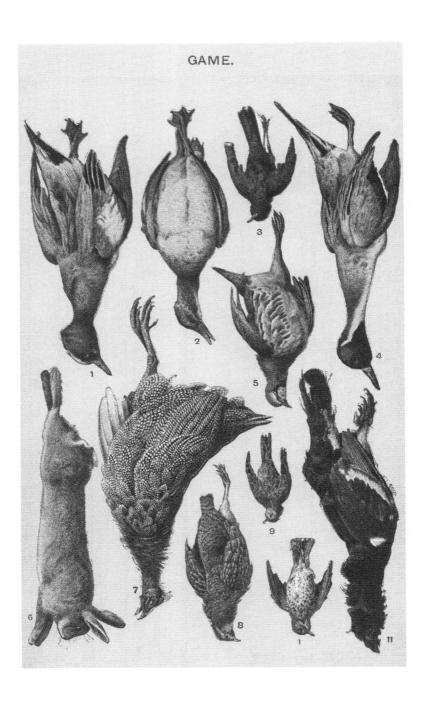

THE RABBIT'S FOOT

by Stephen Dean Ingram

Arkansas 1977

Adam climbed into his seat in the Whirl-A-Wheel. He looked up at the carny seating him, back bowed severely, acne-scarred sunken cheeks, lank hair tucked behind his ears. A pack of cigarettes bulged from one rolled-up sleeve of the man's black t-shirt, its back sunbleached to gray. At the carny's hip a chain looped from a knot of keys. An amber-colored rattlesnake rattle dangled by the keys, next to it a faded white rabbit's foot, a soft contrast to the hardness of the chiseled metal and snake tail. He glanced sideways at Adam as he slammed down the safety bar to his lap, the keys jangling sharply at his waist.

Adam smoothed his hands along the steel bar and looked behind him. His cousins Dickie and Foy plopped down into their seats and cranked down their bar themselves. Dickie was the older cousin, bandy-legged with dark curly hair, always moving, always talking. He wore a turquoise western shirt, pearl buttons, sleeves rolled up to the elbows, tight Wranglers. Foy was Dickie's younger brother, lighter haired, taller than Dickie, doughy. His tan velour shirt stretched tight, pink lower belly exposed, jeans hanging loosely from a flat butt. Foy had a habit of staring at strangers and smiling gap-mouthed, head lowered, as if mulling some peril. Adam didn't know if Foy did it for fun, or if he even knew he was doing it. Adam's mother always said Foy wasn't quite right.

Foy kicked Adam's seatback. "Stop it," said Adam. Foy kicked it harder.

Dickie grabbed Adam by the shoulders from behind. "Doin' okay, cuz?"

"Yeah."

"Good." He released Adam's shoulders. "Hey, look at her," Dickie, grinning, said to Foy. A girl in painted-on white jeans sauntered past them on the midway below. A purple plastic comb handle jutted from her back pocket, the comb's teeth visible through the thin denim. She had dirty dishwater blonde hair and was eating a corn dog. A dab of mustard edged her lips. Their eyes followed her closely as she passed.

"I want me some of that," said Dickie. Foy chortled. "Let's go!" shouted Dickie, bouncing his fists on the bar. The carny ignored him and continued to seat customers. Once everyone was seated, the carny yanked a long steel lever. The Whirl-A-Wheel shuddered as its gears engaged, the seats bouncing, and then began to slowly rotate.

***

Dickie and Foy were from Fort Smith. They weren't really city kids but they weren't really country, either. Their family was down for the weekend, visiting the grandmother the boys shared with Adam.

Their grandma's place was 40 acres of oak and brambles in the Ouachita Mountains backing down to a hollow, crowned by a four-room stone and tar paper house. Five rooms if you counted the bathroom add-on from 1960. The house faced up to the county road that ran along the spine of a ridge. Adam could remember when the road wasn't paved, a plume of dust tailing up from their Impala as they made the annual pilgrimage into the mountains. His father didn't come with them that summer. He usually didn't. He didn't hunt, he didn't fish, wasn't an outdoor kind of guy. So Adam didn't grow up hunting and fishing, didn't know how to skin a squirrel or gut a perch or clean a shotgun. Which weren't necessary skills at home. But he wasn't home.

Adam and his mother were spending July there. The flatland heat of Dallas was exchanged for soggy Arkansas swelter. Clouds of tiny black insects encircled Adam's head and chiggers invaded his privates. He slapped the air and scratched himself constantly.

For his cousins, their grandma's place was some sort of playground for loosened inhibitions. They were older than

Adam and let him know it. When they went down to the swimming hole in the Cossatot, they told Adam to jump in first, which made the water moccasins wriggle away from their nest on the far side of the river. Foy skipped stones on the river surface to try to hit the snakes, the shiny black ripples accelerating away from the barrage. They made Adam light the wad of Black Cat firecrackers they crammed into a wooden fencepost fronting the road while they stayed back around the corner of the barn. Adam lit the fuse and ran for his life. The explosion shredded the top of the post and drove a splinter into the back of his head. The only time he had fired a gun was when Dickie goaded him into pointing a .22 rifle straight up at a buzzard circling above their grandma's old barn. The buzzard was unharmed, Adam's shoulder bruised.

Adam's mother was born and raised in that house and settled easily back into the rhythms of country life. Biscuits with eggs fried in an iron skillet in a chunk of leftover bacon grease scooped from an old coffee can, eaten before dawn. Tomatoes and blackberries picked in the morning, the sizzle of summer insects swelling in the air. Naps taken in the mid-day heat in the back room. Black-eyed peas shelled on the front porch, his grandmother's calloused bare feet skiffing across the concrete porch floor rhythmically as she flicked the peas into a large plastic bowl.

Adam could never get used to those rhythms. He didn't wake until mid-morning in his squeaky steel-springed bed in the back room, wasps pinging off the inside of the corrugated metal roof above. His grandma scoffed as he shuffled wild-haired into the kitchen and grabbed a cold biscuit from a skillet sitting on the stovetop. When sent out for berry picking, he bent over awkwardly to the thorny brambles. He hurriedly filled his bucket, fingers inked with blackberry juice, on the watch for thick rustlings in the emerald tangle of foliage around his feet.

Dickie and Foy would sometimes be sent out to grab a chicken for dinner from the small chicken house out back. Their grandma stood in the yard and dispatched it with a forceful twist of the wrist and plucked it quickly with rough pulls of the hand, the brothers chucking each other on the shoulder in awe as they watched. But the brothers otherwise had no patience for staying around the house. In the afternoons they took off with their grandma's shotgun, squirrels or highway signs the target. After dinner they took off with a case of 3.2 beer they got across the border in the nearest "wet" county in Oklahoma, girls or trouble the target.

The Vandervoort Fair was in the adjacent town, the summer's only organized entertainment in that part of the county. Dickie and Foy asked Adam to go to the fair with them that night. Adam was flattered. They never included him in their outings. His mother ironed a shirt for him to wear. He was happy to escape the tedium of another evening spent sitting on the scalloped metal chairs out on the front porch, the night air pulsing with chirping frogs and insects, as his grandma held forth on the chances of rain and her opinions of the neighbors' children. Myrtie's son couldn't hold a job and was "no account."

The Russell girl had to get married, she's working at the Piggly Wiggly in DeQueen, that boy who knocked her up got a job at the Grannis chicken plant.

They drove to the fair in Dickie's purple pickup. Adam was wedged between Dickie and Foy on the bench seat, arms squeezed together on top of his legs. A chicken truck sped ahead, the fryers sitting in plastic crates stacked six high on the flatbed trailer. White feathers from the crates flew up and dotted the twilight sky.

"The chicken in the middle of those crates is always dead by the time they get to the plant," said Dickie. "Sucks for it." Adam was nauseous as they bobbed up and down the mountain road, Dickie gunning the motor periodically for effect, Uriah Heep blaring from the eight-track.

They parked in the field next to the fairgrounds, comprised of a double row of booths, a half dozen rides, a stock car track, and scattered trailers. As they left the ticket booth, Dickie winked at Adam and showed him his tooled leather wallet with a condom inserted inside. There was a circle impression on the outside of the wallet. "Gotta always be ready," Dickie said. Adam had never seen one outside of the boxes placed out of reach behind the drugstore counter. He nodded to Dickie, but felt uneasy, and wondered what else he had in mind for the night.

***

The Whirl-A-Wheel ride ended. Adam walked down

the stairs from the ride platform. Dickie got out of his seat and scooped up something laying on the platform. He and Foy jumped off together and landed on the ground next to Adam. Dickie and Foy chuckled to themselves. The three of them meandered down the midway, looking at the games. The naked lightbulbs framing the game booths punctuated the inky blackness of the surrounding woods.

As they walked away, the carny felt at his waist and jerked his head around as he scanned the rusted deck. "Where the goddamn hell is it?"

The stock car track at the Vandervoort Fair was a bladed red-clay bowl, its top pushed up above ground level. A procession of stock cars rode up and over the top of the bowl and slid down into the track, battered remnants of old sedans pieced together: a dun-colored fender with a Ford insignia hammered onto a Dodge, a Studebaker with a Chevy trunk wired on, Bondo smeared here and there. The driver's door of each car bore a hand-painted number. Wooden bleachers abutted one side of the track. The track announcer's voice crackled from a single speaker hanging off the plywood-sided press box affixed to the top of the stands. Four or five cars at a time furiously ringed the inside of the steeply-graded bowl, churning up a cloud of red dust which hung in the air over the track. A checkered flag appeared. The racers disappeared over the lip of the bowl into the darkness.

Adam stood under the stands with Dickie and Foy. Bands of light peeked through the stands and illuminated russet dust motes floating down from above. Foy held a jar of moonshine Dickie bought from a sorghum farmer they met in the stands. Foy took a long draught, dribbling some on his shirt. He wiped his lips with the sweatband on his wrist and handed the jar to Adam. "Here you go," he said, eyes glazed, and let out a loud burp.

Adam held the jar with both hands, hesitated, and slowly brought it to his lips. It smelled like the can of turpentine in their garage at home. "Go on, try it," said Foy, and grinned at Dickie. Adam drank, more than he meant to, and winced as the corn liquor raged down his throat. Dickie slapped Foy on the back and they both laughed. Tears squeezed out of the corners of Adam's eyes.

Dickie reached for the jar. "Burns, don't it?" he said. "Alright, we've got something for you." Dickie pulled something out of his front pocket and held it out to Adam. It was a rabbit's foot, its color dusky in the shadows of the bleachers.

"Where'd you get that?" said Adam.

"Found it," said Dickie. "Finders, keepers. Anyway, you take it. A rabbit's foot is good luck."

"You sure?" said Adam. Where had he seen a rabbit's foot that night?

"Course I'm sure. Here." Dickie clipped the rabbit's foot to Adam's beltloop and backed away. "Cool." Adam twisted around and looked at the foot, now attached to him, and fingered its rounded claws.

Woozy from the moonshine, Adam stayed at the track

to watch the races for a while. Dickie and Foy went back to the midway. Adam sat away from the other spectators on the highest plank of the bleachers. The drone of the announcer's voice and the steady churn of the engines below lulled him into a stupor. Random visions appeared in his daydream: girls in tight jeans, headless chickens, snarling dogs with bared teeth. He stirred from his reverie when the last race of the night ended and everyone started moving out of the stands.

Adam idled his way back down the midway, looking for Dickie and Foy. He couldn't find them and stopped at a game booth to kill some time. It was the one with the water guns where you race to fill your balloon first.

A large clown face was painted on the back wall of the booth, below it a row of nozzles to which flaccid balloons were attached. The clown leered at those standing before it, its eyes arched and angry, belying its clumsy smile.

Adam waited for the signal to begin shooting. He never won at these games. He gripped the water gun tightly, slightly bent over. The Whirl-A-Wheel was on the opposite side of the midway from the booth, its mechanism now still. A bell signaled the start of the game. Adam kept his eyes on the brass nozzle he was shooting at. The pink balloon attached to his nozzle rose faster than the others. Maybe he was going to win something this time. His balloon grew fatter, and fatter, and popped first.

"We have a winner," said the man running the booth, pointing to Adam. The other contestants groaned and drifted away.

"Hey!" said a voice behind Adam, barely distinct from the rest of the midway chatter.

As a prize he could choose one of two stuffed animals, a fuzzy green parrot or a blue elephant. "I guess I'll take the parrot," Adam said to the man.

Adam was jerked around by his shoulder. His parrot dropped to the soda-wetted grass. The carny from the Whirl-A-Wheel stood before him. "Hey! Didn't you hear me? Where'd you get that?" the carny said, pointing to the rabbit's foot hanging off of Adam's beltloop. Which Adam had completely forgotten about until that moment.

"I—found it," Adam stammered. "I mean, my friend—my cousin found it."

"Bullshit." The carny held the front of Adam's shirt in his fist and looked around quickly, then pushed him backward around the booth and into the dark woods immediately beyond. He shoved Adam up against a pine tree. The rough resiny bark dug into Adam's back. The sounds of the midway seemed far away.

The carny yanked the rabbit's foot away from Adam and held it up to his face. "Do you know what this is? My granddaddy gave me this when I was little. I always keep it with me. And I'm tired of you little shits from town thinking you can just come out here and take whatever you want. Is that what you think? Huh?" He mashed Adam harder up against the tree trunk. Adam, wide-eyed, couldn't speak. He clawed at the air to try to steady himself. His muscles tightened, and

Adam was keenly aware of the sounds of keys jingling and bark scraping. He felt something pull loose from the carny in the struggle and held it beside him in a gripped hand, afraid to let go of whatever it was.

Adam had never been in a fight, didn't know how to fight. A boy in freshman PE class once claimed he cheated on a tennis score and pushed him against a locker, wanting to fight. Adam froze. The boy cursed him and walked away. Now he was being challenged again.

The carny's fist tightened, knuckles pressing harder into his chest each time he squirmed. "You wanna lesson, boy?" said the carny. "Is that what you want?" He reached around behind him, jerked his hand sideways and held up a switchblade, its blade shimmering from the midway lights lacing into the forest. Adam panicked at the sight of the knife. His right knee jerked upward sharply of its own accord into the carny's crotch, his kneebone smashing its contents like a ripe tomato dropped onto a concrete floor. The carny howled, dropped the knife and collapsed onto the forest floor, rolling side to side among the pine needles.

Adam remained pressed to the tree. Foy lumbered out of the deeper woods and stood before them taking in the scene. He looked down, saw the knife laying in the pine needles and picked it up. He winked at Adam, turned to the carny and kicked him hard in the stomach. The carny shrieked.

"I wasn't gonna do nothin', was just gonna scare 'im," he moaned, and then melted into the ground, mumbling. Adam finally stepped away from the tree, shaking, fists clenched.

Foy chuckled. "Lez go," he said to Adam, who looked back at the carny as they walked toward the midway lights.

Dickie emerged from the woods behind them, pulling at his jeans, which were unzipped and riding around his hips. The dirty dishwater blonde girl followed him out, adjusting the top of her blouse.

"Hey, I was just—takin' care of some business," said Dickie, smirking at the girl, who looked back at him with a wan smile as she strolled away. "We heard all the commotion. Saw that asshole on the ground back there. What happened?"

Foy twirled the knife in his hand for Dickie to see and nodded back to the woods.

Dickie looked to Adam. "Damn! You okay? That sumbitch didn't cut you, did he?"

"No," said Adam. "I'm okay."

"Well, I guess you are." Dickie grinned. "Look at you, now. Kicked his ass, looks like."

Adam looked down and shrugged. "He wanted his rabbit's foot."

"He did? Christ, all that over a goddamn rabbit's foot? Hey, good thing Foy was keeping lookout for me, we might not of saw you there."

"Good thing," said Adam.

"But I guess you got it handled, didn't you?" Dickie clapped Adam on the shoulder. Adam blushed.

The headlights illuminated the black oaks and slash pines

lining the county road as they drove home. The churn of the pickup's engine echoed off the forest walls. Dickie gave Adam the seat by the window this time.

Dickie crowed about the night's events. "Best night ever," he said. "And Adam, man, that girl had a friend, but we couldn't find you."

"I was still at the track," said Adam.

"Your loss. Hey, don't tell our mamas about all this, okay? This is just between us." Dickie looked over to Adam, eyebrows raised expectantly.

"Of course, yeah," said Adam.

"Good man. Anyway, too bad about that rabbit's foot," said Dickie. "Bad luck, I guess."

"I guess," said Adam, as he looked down at his left hand. The carny's snake rattle lay in his palm, amber and blood-streaked. He held it up close to his ear and shook it. The menace of its high-pitched clatter was contained in his hand.

Adam rolled down his window and let the wind blast his face. He leaned his forehead out and looked at the night sky, the stars shining from a veil of black velvet darkness, unclouded by ambient city light. He hadn't really noticed how brilliant the country sky was before.

UNDER A NEW MOON

by Chella Courington

In a room without corners, she walked in circles. Why? She wasn't sure. When a child, she'd noticed that her Dachshund circled his pallet before settling down to rest. But then his ancestors were wolves who paced round and round a spot, stamping the leaves and grass to carve out their nest. But in a renovated grain silo in the now hip industrial East Side, her abode stayed ready—a space of clean surfaces with a desk, small refrigerator, convection oven, and bed in the middle. Long before lying down, she moved in circles and left black skids on bamboo. Their diameter rarely varied. She always wore running shoes in case she needed a quick exit. In a city a woman alone was prey. Some nights she slept in her Nikes, and every morning she washed her floors.

Thursday after eating a banana while drinking an espresso, she read that a German scientist had dropped subjects in an unfamiliar forest during the day and during the night to see whether they would proceed in rings when lost. After tracking them with a Global Positioning System, the scientist had reported: *If the sun or moon was out, they were able to move straight ahead. Yet if it was completely dark or even cloudy, they ambulated in a 360-degree path, just a few hundred yards across.*

She put the newspaper in her recycle bin (another object in the room) and stood still. Waiting. She saw the Sahara with its sand and shallow basins. If dropped there, she would never be able to get farther than a quarter of a mile from where she began. Her eyes felt grainy, her mouth dry. Leaving her room today would be impossible. Why would she, knowing how easy it was to lose her way at home, ever trust the linear grid of sidewalks and streets to guide her where she wanted to go?

BLUE HOUR

by Chella Courington

The street below was almost empty. Neither daylight nor complete darkness. Alone on the balcony, she dipped her fingers in the dregs of cabernet. She had told him—*Don't come back if you smell of the whore's cheap perfume.* Seven days later, he had not returned. A man who was between her legs for a fortnight. Eager as a child learning to swim. He spoke of living and dying together on a beach near Venice, their years mere moments. And then it happened. Notes floated up from the past, pulling him back to a woman who shattered his heart and pushed him adrift. The whore found his pieces and washed them in sweet water before drying in the sun. Asking nothing, wanting nothing except a few gold coins.

DESTINATION UNKNOWN

by Max Talley

Ward Christian stirred his coffee. Tasted awful, so he drank more. *Not enough sugar, cream?* Phones had been ringing all morning but his recent promotion meant that others screened callers and only transferred serious complaints to him. He worked for Gore-Blarg, the stupid name for waste management in Santa Maya—a coastal town seventy miles north of Los Angeles.

The light blinked on his line, a clunky phone of late '80s vintage. "Good Morning. Gore-Blarg Solutions here. How can I help you today?"

"Who am I speaking to?"

"This is Ward, uh, Christian."

"Great, this is Albert, Atheist."

"No, I'm not—"

"Whatever. Is this illegal dumping?"

"Well, I handle related complaints."

"I live on the 3100 Block of Upper Main Street. Someone left a big couch outside between two apartment complexes."

"And that's bothering you?" Ward had been told to use a therapist voice, to calm and soothe troubled callers. Some being daily nuisances, cranks with no life.

"Yes, it's blocking the sidewalk. Have to walk into traffic to get around it. That's dangerous. Plus, it's an ugly color and looks...moist."

"I can send a truck out within 24 hours."

"Thank you," Albert said. "You're a decent garbage man."

"I'm not a garbage man." His voice rose. "I am in Waste Management and Retrieval Coordination." Ward stopped when he realized Albert had disconnected. He filled out a retrieval order, noting that Hernandez and Wilcox covered Upper Main. He put the request in the computer system, but also left cards in the men's boxes they checked when signing-in and signing-out.

His cute assistant Gloria buzzed on another 20th century device, his intercom.

"There's a call from a Jennifer Tucker," Gloria said. "She sounds familiar."

"That's Jen, my wife." He hesitated. "Can we have a drink after work, Gloria?"

"Oh, so she didn't take your last name?"

"Um, no." Ward crushed a piece of scrap paper in his hand. "Please put her through."

"Hi, darling," Jen said. "How are you doing?"

"Since I saw you two hours ago? Fine." He stared at the window. "Was there something important?"

"They delivered it."

"What?"

"The new bidet. Installed and everything. Marci says it's a life-changing experience."

"Marci?"

"Online sales manager. But she'll continue as our contact, to guide us through the first month of use." Jen let out a satisfied gasp. "I feel so continental."

Ward yawned. "That's fantastic, honey. I really need to get back to work."

"Of course. When you get your next promotion we can buy the Jacuzzi tub."

***

Ben Wilcox and Victor Hernandez received the pick-up request at 9 a.m. Victor felt relieved they no longer rode on giant stinking garbage trucks, nor did they wear the stained jumpsuit uniforms. Instead of bags of rotting trash, they merely hefted furniture into a hauling truck.

When they reached the 3100 block of Upper Main Street, car traffic was dense, but few pedestrians strolled the sidewalk.

Victor looked up and down the gentle slope, then spotted

it in all its hideous purple glory. "There she blows." Ben found a nearby parking spot, alleviating blocking a traffic lane.

The sofa stretched a good seven feet. Definitely a two-man job. Ben took the end jutting across the sidewalk and Victor grabbed the side tucked into the alley between neighboring apartment complexes. The material felt spongy to the touch, weird. "One, two, and lift," Victor shouted.

Ben levered it up, but shuddered from the strain. "Gah, my back." He dropped his end. "I drank two Tornadoes at Jerry's Pub last night. Exhausted today." A hand pressed to his forehead seemed to be holding him up. "How much time we got for this job?"

"An hour," Victor replied. "Maybe used ten minutes so far."

"Listen, let me take a nap for a half-hour. We'll still reach the city dump in time."

"Nap? Where?"

"On the couch, dummy. Looks comfortable."

"Yeah, I don't get why no one snagged this for their home, or to sell at a thrift store." Victor scanned the blur of cars passing as if for some authority to decide. "Okay. But let's push it into the alley so it doesn't obstruct foot traffic."

"Fine with me," Ben said. "Out of the sun's glare."

Though heavy to lift, strangely, it slid easily back into the shaded alleyway. "What do I do for thirty minutes?"

"Get some coffee or go on Instagram, or you know, the Mexican version of Facebook."

"You mean...Facebook?" Victor turned, but Ben had

already stretched out with a forearm over his eyes. So he walked uphill and bought a $5 iced coffee at the Bean Dream.

After twenty minutes, Victor grew paranoid. There could be traffic delays on the way to the dump, and if a supervisor should drive by and catch them dawdling, they'd go right back to slop truck duty.

"Ben?" Their vehicle remained parked in the same place, but the couch sat empty. "Ben?" Victor scoped the alley, patrolled the street, but found no sign of his partner. He did notice Ben's glazed doughnut propped on an armrest. The seat cushions seemed to undulate, for a moment looking porous, then gelatinous.

Victor picked a three-foot palm frond off the sidewalk and pressed it to the sofa's base. It went slowly through the material, sinking from sight. When less than a foot remained, Victor pulled back. But it was stuck. Then, something within yanked, dragging the frond into the seat cushion, as well as Victor's hand. "Shit. Let go!" He felt chilled, flesh numb. Finally he extricated his hand and stared at it. The skin blurred, went lighter then darker, came in and out of focus. *Leave now.* Victor jumped into the truck and returned to Gore-Blarg headquarters at high speed.

***

Ward woke up feeling weary. His wife chattered on her phone, sometimes singing bits of awful pop songs. "You're beautiful, beautiful."

"I slept terribly," he told her. "The full moon disrupts my sleep cycle."

"The moon doesn't go full till next week, silly," Jen said.

"Well, it's beginning to. I need black-out curtains, like Elvis had at Graceland."

"FYI, Elvis died at forty-two." Jen chuckled. "I just spent a half-hour on the bidet," she added. "There's a wide-spray setting that gently firms and tones your butt-cheeks."

"Great." Ward staggered to the bathroom. He squatted on La Royale 4000 and relaxed. A video screen to the side buzzed on. "Welcome, occupant. I'm Marci, here to facilitate you through your new purchase."

Ward grabbed at his pants by his ankles. "You can see me?"

"Of course not, I'm A.I.," Marci replied.

"Oh, good."

"However, we have human operatives in Sumatra and Taiwan who are monitoring this product whenever in use."

Ward jumped up. The release of weight on the seat switched the screen off with a static fizz. After his ablutions, he drank coffee to wash down the burned scrambled eggs and English muffins, then rushed to work.

The office gave him no peace. His team hadn't retrieved the purple couch. Then more complaints: a green sofa on Upper Main and a chaise lounge on Lower Main. Ward hadn't heard that term in years. Sort of a daybed. You could nap on one, but not quite sleep on it like a big couch. The last caller sounded familiar.

"Albert, again?"

"Uh-huh," he whispered. "The couches aren't what they seem."

"What?"

"They're fancy-looking, leather and suede. Quality furniture usually gets nabbed fast by passersby. People come look, but never take them."

"Why haven't you, Albert?"

"Something odd. It's a conspiracy, I tell you..."

Ward hung up. Gloria buzzed him before noon.

"Can we have lunch together?"

"No," she said. "One of your retrieval men is here waiting for you."

"In person?" The whole point of having a private office was not to see workers, to hide away from all corporate bullshit and just slither through the day. "Okay, send him in." Ward's irritation distracted him from asking who it was.

A white-haired Latino man shuffled into the office with his head bowed.

"Hector Garcia?" Ward said. "Didn't we plan to discuss your retirement next month, when you turn sixty-five?"

"I'm thirty-five, Mr. Christian." He raised his face to glance at Ward.

"Victor? Holy shit, what happened to your hair? And where's Wilcox?"

Victor described the morning and Ben's disappearance.

Ward paced the room. "You believe he sank into the couch,

got swallowed? Have you been drinking? I know microdosing is popular these days but I didn't think it crossed into your community."

Victor pulled his right hand out of his pocket for Ward to see. The man's brown skin had been bleached white. "It got wet inside the couch. Is numb, no feeling."

Ward felt sudden fear. Not of the unknown, but of lawsuits directed at Gore-Blarg. Upper management would blame him. He had to act on instinct; logic made no sense. "Victor, take the rest of the day off." He offered two twenties from his wallet. "Treat your wife to dinner." He sighed. "A temporary condition. Clorox liquid bleach leaked inside a seat cushion and did that. Get some rest. Tomorrow we'll be joking about this." Ward forced a laugh but Victor showed only a sickly smile as he hobbled out of the office.

Gloria buzzed again. "It's Preston Crasburn from the University Club."

"I'll call back."

"Says either you speak to him or he'll go to the General Manager."

"Okay," he said. "Preston, long time no see."

"Ward, I've been tooling around Santa Maya, and discarded sofas are littering the streets. I show our fair city to a preservation committee on Friday. How will they react? Not well, I tell you."

"The matter was just brought to my attention. I'm dealing with it."

"Really?" Preston made a sound best described as a

harrumph. "Don't you realize, beds and couches are magnets for the homeless population. They sleep on them, fornicate on them, perhaps even—"

"Have you seen any houseless people on the couches?"

"Houseless? Is that the current preferred term?"

"Today's Tuesday," Ward said. "I'll clear it up by Friday."

"We wouldn't want this to jeopardize your application to the University Club."

"No, no. Thanks for your concern, Preston."

Ward contacted Tug McGraw and Lonnie Wilson. Big lugs who'd worked on the drilling platforms offshore. "It's not your area, but I need this purple couch picked up ASAP. There's extra money in it for you. Plus, kudos from the old man upstairs."

He instructed all calls to be held then took a nap on the office carpeting. Impossible erotic dreams about Gloria ensued. As if being married wasn't enough, Ward was her superior and any pass he made could be reported, seen as workplace harassment. In his reveries, she was his boss—demanding physical favors.

The buzzer sounded over and over, waking him. "What is it?"

"A retrieval man. Says it's urgent." Gloria transferred him.

"Mr. Christian? Lonnie here. Couch was heavy as hell. Wouldn't move. I went to hook up the winch and when I got back..."

"Yes, yes?"

"Tug McGraw was gone. He couldn't have run off."

"Where are you?"

"In the truck on Upper Main, waiting for him to show."

"I'm coming down."

Ward parked his Kia Sedona at the corner of the 3100 block and tapped on the utility truck's passenger window. "Did Tug come back?"

"Nope."

"Never had someone walk off the job." *Except Ben Wilcox.* Ward rolled up his sleeves. "Okay, let's haul that thing over."

"Are you sure?" Lonnie brushed back his greasy mop. "At your age?"

"I'm fifty."

"No, really?"

"Well, fifty-five, but I feel fifty." Ward moved into the alley, leaned over, and shoved the couch, while Lonnie pulled it toward where the winch hook could attach. Ward grunted and groaned, straining for what seemed like five minutes, then looked up. "Did it move?"

"Maybe an inch."

"This isn't some valuable antique. Do you keep hammers in the truck?"

"Of course." Lonnie smiled before retrieving two sledgehammers.

"You piece of crap," Ward said. They swung at the couch, striking it over and over. The armrests soon broke off and finally the back frame collapsed, leaving the base. They only hit the seat cushions twice before both burst open. A thick black liquid oozed out. It bubbled and steamed like hot oil.

"Step back away from that," Ward yelled.

As a former boxer and linebacker, Lonnie had taken multiple hits to the head and his brain functioned a tad slower. When the liquid slime drenched his boots, he roused from a trance and jumped back. A loud hissing sounded and smoke rose. "Ow, it's burning hot."

"Take your boots off—now!"

Lonnie obeyed. He hurled them away and the pair soon dissolved as if soaked in acid, leaving only a rubbery stench in the air. "Holy fuck," he said.

The dark liquid pooled together then gushed out into a storm drain. The couch frame and cushions had dissolved too. Soon the alley sat empty beyond the stunned men. Children peered from windows in adjacent apartments, mouths agape.

***

Later that afternoon, Ward got summoned upstairs. Tyler Johnson was thirty-five, and had been installed as Acting Manager by his father Cyrus, President of Gore-Blarg.

The spacious office held no desk and Tyler skateboarded around it when Ward entered.

"Dude, thanks for showing. The old man's all up in my business."

"About what?"

"Street furniture. Missing employees." Tyler leaped off his skateboard and slid on knee pads across the wooden floor.

He stood to fist-bump Ward. "Also, homeless people been vanishing for a week." Tyler grinned like a simpleton. "I mean that's cool, because, you know, but it's uncool, because these local organizations are like outraged. I told them, it is what it is, but that didn't soothe them, man. I told them, it's all good, and they said, no, it's all bad."

"Not my fault."

"I feel ya." Tyler nodded. "But if the blame has to land on you or me, yeah, it's totally your fault."

Ward couldn't share what he'd witnessed earlier. "I didn't know we had a responsibility to the houseless population."

"Neither did I." Tyler lit a bowl of weed in a glass pipe. "City thinks we're leaving quality couches and beds out in public and that's luring homeless people from shelters to live on the streets." He coughed. "The shelters need to show their numbers, amount of people they help and feed, to get their state money and shit." He put his hands up in exasperation. "Dad's hassling me, but I'm traumatized by blame. So I have to pass this on to you, bro. If you can't make things happen, it's down the elevator shaft."

"You'd do that?"

"Nah. Cyrus would. Good news is you're still working, but in a deep dank space, alone." He flashed a knowing smile. "No hot assistant, like Gloria."

***

At dinner, Ward and Jen continued their argument about a

monthly date night. Ward campaigned that it should be twice a month.

"You told me your married buds don't have any sex." Jen's fake eyelashes flared outward. "So you're getting twelve times as much as they are. I'd prefer less though. Sometimes Winky just doesn't feel up to it."

Ward woke up twice during the night to ramble about the bedroom.

Jen muttered, "You're bothering me. Go read a book on the bidet."

"The full moon is glaring in here. I see the light and think it's early morning. Throwing off my natural rhythms."

She grumbled her way out of bed to pull open the shades facing Main Street. "No moon, see?" Jen pointed. "It's that streetlamp. The metal hood came off and it's shining this way." She slumped back onto the mattress.

Ward wrapped a towel around his head and finally dozed off.

The next day, he enlisted the six remaining retrieval men to help. "Guys, don't try to remove couches or sofas. Instead, hide them, tuck them into alleyways, behind dumpsters. Slide them away from street view. Everything else, wooden chairs, book cases, desks, you'll haul to the dump. If Upper and Lower Main look clean by Friday, there's a bonus in it."

"What about Ben, and Tug McGraw?"

Ward sniffed. "They'll be back. Mark my words."

"You don't think they got munched on, eaten up?" Victor

asked, a glove on his right hand.

"Of course not. That's crazy talk."

***

Through some miracle, Ward's plan worked. Friday, when he drove the five miles of Main Street, he didn't spot a single couch or any furniture. Not one trash complaint call came through Gloria either.

He had a solo drink after work then went home. Lights were blazing and dance music throbbed, while cars filled most parking spots. *Crap, I forgot.* Jen's cocktail party to impress the town snobs. She being a social climber. They lived on the 4000 block of Main Street, the top of the hill. Not an expensive cottage, but the best apartment view over the city and toward the distant ocean.

Ward entered their living room crowded with twenty people. "You're late." Jen lightly elbowed him. "Guess what? The new bidet is a big hit."

He quickly changed into a fresh shirt and jacket. When he mixed a drink, Preston Crasburn sidled up. "Congratulations, Bubby. I gave my tour today and your area looked near perfect." He fingered the university crest on his blazer. "Not only did you dispose of the unsightly furniture," Preston switched to a booze-flavored whisper in Ward's ear, "but the homeless population was invisible." He stepped back. "Continue that magic and a spot on the city council awaits—"

"Thanks, but what about University Club membership?"

Ward said. "Jen keeps harping on it. Says we're nobodies if we can't join."

"Your chances at the U.C. rose dramatically today." Preston's voice caught in his throat. "It's just the garbage man thing."

"I'm not a garbage man," Ward insisted. "My job title is, Human Resources—Waste Management." He proffered his business card.

Preston nodded with a pained smile. "Cards are so 1998. Everything's online. When members look you up—as they will—your title's been simplified." Preston flashed his giant pulsing iPhone 14 and tapped Gore-Blarg personnel. "See?"

It read: *Ward Christian—Human Waste Handler.*

"Our blue blood members are very germ-conscious," Preston continued. "They don't want to shake hands with a chap who's knee-deep in human waste..."

"But I'm not."

"Appearance trumps reality, my friend." He gripped Ward's shoulder. "Just get promoted to Disposal Solutions or Object Transfer. Or Recycling. People love separating their cardboard and plastic. Even if most isn't actually recycled, citizens like to think they're helping the planet by doing almost nothing." He lightly punched Ward's arm. "Get 'er done."

***

Ward returned to Gore-Blarg at 9:15 Monday. He greeted Gloria. "I thought about you this weekend. Will you see me after work?"

"You know we can't. Company policy."

"What if we were in different departments?"

"Um, Mr. Christian, Cyrus is waiting for you on a Zoom call." Gloria trembled a little. "Major Johnson."

Ward hurried into his office and joined the Zoom. A mottled seventy-five-year-old face filled the screen. Due to the low camera angle, Ward gazed up through his chins, seeing the white hairs in Cyrus's flared nostrils, then his red-veined eyes.

"Hello, Mr. Johnson."

"Call me Major." The man had served in food distribution during the five-day invasion of Grenada nearly forty years earlier, though no official documentation of his title could be located.

"I'm hoping my recent achievements might earn me a promotion," Ward said.

Cyrus let out a choking cough, his complexion reddening. "Achievement? Sorry, I'm demoting you."

"Why, sir?"

"Thirty homeless men and six women have vanished. There are photos of several of them sleeping on couches you failed to deliver to the city dump. Those images were posted on the Nextdoor app by annoyed residents. The same transients disappeared soon after."

"Isn't that good?"

"Personally, you're my hero. But from a business point of view, it's disastrous. Civic groups, community organizers are all hounding me. Why are we providing bedding for the homeless and what are we doing with them? I've insisted it was a computer error, but they want heads to roll."

"I don't know what happened to the missing people."

"Jesus, Christian. During the Spanish Inquisition, or fascist Italy, they'd be building statues of you, but here in the socialist republic of California, they care more about the lower rungs of our society than the breadwinners. Like me. I pulled myself up from the bootstraps of my parents' wealth to make Gore-Blarg what it is today." Cyrus pressed so close, his screen face blurred into a pink, wrinkled landscape.

"Transfer me to recycling?" Ward tried not to sound desperate.

Cyrus grunted. "You sure? We don't just recycle bottles and cardboard. It's big stuff now. Machinery, objects, pretty much everything."

"Please, I want that."

"Done. Empty out your desk by noon. Victor Hernandez replaces you."

"Victor?"

"When pressed to the wall by lawyers, we believe in diversity."

***

Days passed in a blur. Ward descended in the freight elevator to Sub-Basement C, below the furnace rooms, beneath the storage decks. He sat at a desk in a cavernous space. The antiquated boxy computer he used to input recycling statistics didn't have an Internet connection. No signal could reach so deep. Twenty feet above, lines of fluorescent light strips buzzed and sometimes fizzled out. Dark shapes the size of small dogs scuttled about the dim far corners. Much of the vast area was taken up by towering stacks of couches, divans, and mattresses. Across the basement, an automatic metal door sometimes slid open and workers took furniture out, perhaps to prop on the sidewalks of Santa Maya. The disheveled men wore ratty clothes and showed long, dirty hair.

At one point, Ward recognized two guys hauling mattresses. "Ben Wilcox, is that you?" No response. "Tug McGraw, I'm glad you're okay."

Both acted like zombies. They briefly stared at Ward without recognition, eyes glazed, both cadaverously pale. He began to understand. The whole conspiracy larger than anyone might imagine.

A mail chute delivered sandwiches in brown paper bags at lunch hour. Ward could leave at 5 p.m. when the elevator arrived. Ringing for it earlier proved fruitless. Up high, near the light strips and clanking pipes sat a metal balcony—only accessible from the next level. One morning as Ward typed endlessly, he heard high heels tapping and squinted upward.

"Gloria, you came to see me."

"I had an errand to do. Wondered what was out here."

"We can finally be together," Ward shouted. "Neither one of us has power, can help or hurt the other anymore. We're free now."

"Yes, that's true." A tear formed in Gloria's left eye; she turned and rushed away.

He stopped going home. After the University Club rejected them, Jen had moved to her sister's Pasadena apartment in shame.

Ward lay back on the most comfortable-looking couch. He sank away until his vision became haloed by a rainbow of colors. When he woke, Ward had somehow fused with the giant eye of the streetlamp across from his apartment. It had been trying to warn him, to signal. People were being transformed, composted, recycled into other forms to benefit the city. From this high perch he watched the yellowy orb rise into the night sky and felt like a moon-drunk saint. A desert mystic atop a lonely tower.

Time passed, immeasurable. At some point he became conscious of the neighboring streetlamp blinking on and off—winking at him. Ward plunged his consciousness down into the coils and turbines, the wires and generators until he sensed it was Gloria. She had transitioned too. He rejoiced and thrummed with utility power, showing her his brightest beam. They both sparked, shimmering in the electra-glow of artificial light. Together they might stave off the pitch blackness of their solitary lives.

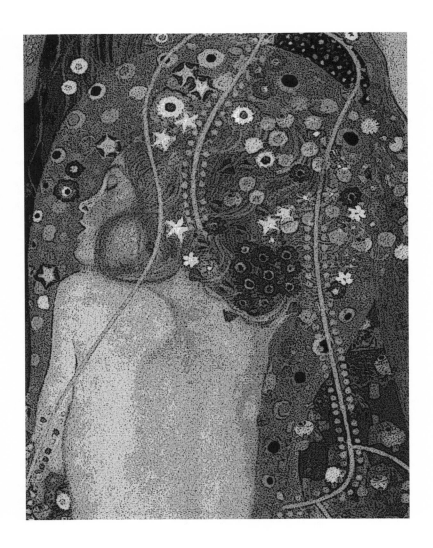

AND SHE LAY THERE
IN THE MOONLIGHT

by Ted Chiles

The night Cindy Palmer walked off the cliff we were drunk and high in The Pit, an old quarry cut back in 1894, creating a hole that resembled the grave of some long dead giant. Our portion of the 1972 graduating class of New Castle High was celebrating with what we could buy, steal, or score. The sun had set, the barely waning moon was out, and Cindy was raging. We'd started without her and she'd found James hitting on Jill. As the evening progressed and supplies dwindled, James tried to smooth it over, but Cindy climbed out, leaving him behind.

We were sorting ourselves into twos when we heard her cry. It wasn't a scream. More like surprised joy, snow on Christmas morning. First orgasm.

It took us five minutes to find her at the bottom of the cliff sprawled across the railroad tracks. James climbed down and I went to call an ambulance. The residual scattered.

Cindy didn't break a bone, but her left kidney split. The doctors said all that she'd smoked and drank kept her from understanding what was happening. Gracing her earlobes were kidney bean earrings. A necklace of the same legumes circled her neck.

Cindy wouldn't show me her scar.

How did it feel? I asked.

Like when my dad tossed me in the air.

***

At our twenty-fifth reunion held at the newer of New Castle's two Holiday Inns, I saw Cindy and James kissing in the parking lot. Locked together like two lovers in Pompeii frozen by the gases and ash of Vesuvius. She went home to Cleveland, packed a suitcase, and left her husband and son. I always wondered, as she lay on the tracks too fucked up to feel the pain, did she think her father had not caught her? That he had let her pass straight through his arms.

ONE DROP OF DEW

by Lori Anaya

One drop of dew on the tip of a leaf
before sunrise,
hangs, sparkles
drops
on a rock
where a lizard sat
in a flash gone to shadows
awaits
an insect
who alights,
sips,
sticks on the quick tongue of the reptile
who in a second of delay
becomes the great egret's snack
before she flies back
to river's edge

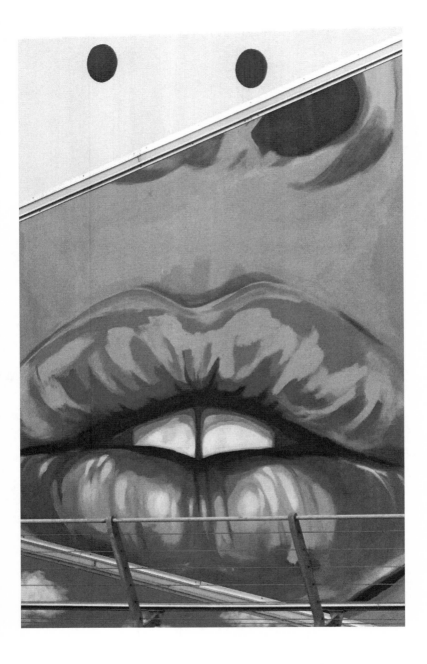

INSOMNIA

by Alexis Rhone Fancher

I wish I could drift off like you do.
You, who sleep like the dead.
Insomniac me, up till dawn.
Watching stars flirt with the moon.

You sleep like the dead.
I wish I could dream like you do,
Instead, I watch stars flirt with the moon.
What's your secret?

Why can't I dream like you do?
Your smile, a dead giveaway.
What's your secret?
The lies you rosary so you can sleep?

Your grin, a dead giveaway.
So goddamn peaceful.
The lies you rosary so you can sleep.
I make do with whisky and pills.

So goddamn peaceful.
Insomniac me, up till dawn.
I resort to whisky and pills.
Why can't I drift off like you do?

SONNET

by Fritz Feltzer

Eleven p.m.
A recent working day.
The words scurry about
like impatient cats who want out,
then yowl
for immediate reentry.
Time to halt
my chase of narrative.
Best to consign the pages
to a night's sleep
and a hope
the Grand Guignol of dreams
offers the relief of words
that do not curdle.

THE VISITING POET

by Fritz Feltzer

Her appointment called for three readings,
a consult with students, judge a contest.
The prize—a manuscript mark-up and an hour's private consult.
She labored through seventeen student submissions,
chose my thesis draft for the prize.
We met in a former janitor's closet
pimped up as an office
for visiting poets and writers.
She's late forties, swaths of gray in an untrimmed
unbraided splash of stage presence, a knobby beanpole,
publishing credits up the wazoo.
Me, too serious for my own poetry,
a badass grad student with exorbitant ego and student debt.
Don't fuck with me or my meter. I got my spondees and dactyls
working.
She'd worn sunglasses to all her readings, big round Warby Parkers,
wore them to my hour consult, not to forget clunky beaded bracelets
platform-soled Doc Martens maryjanes.
She did a fingernail toccata and fugue on the table before she shoved
my manuscript to me, its pages brimming Post-it notes like
sprouty sandwiches at a health food store.
A distinguished visiting poet. Sunglasses. Clunky beads.
Fucking Doc Martens.
"You need—" she began.

No one tells a badass grad student what he needs.

"Get crazy," she said. "Your poems?"

Did she actually say "Hah?" Or did I imagine it?

She pointed to the infection of Post-it notes. "Great meter,
but OMG, the sanity. Read Ernest Dowsen. Read Whatsisname,
puked his guts out on lawns across America."

"Dylan Thomas," I said.

"Proper crazy," she said. Two spondees.

So.

Adios, Bob Browning.

Hasta la vista, Dr. Williams, even though so much depended on that
wheelbarrow.

Abandoned Eliot without so much as a whimper.

Took up Crazy Ez. Didn't Eliot say of him, "*Il miglior fabbro*"?

Wallowed in Crazy Willie, caught the fire in my head.

Tossed caution to the winds with Langston Hughes, wide-open door
to Mary O.

Quit MFA program, thus adios to any potential teaching gig,
spent the next two years on *The Steampunk Cantos*,
sent a copy to the visiting poet.

A week later, an email from her.

"I do not read or comment on materials from former students."

A week later, an apology. She remembered me.

She sent my material to a publisher pal in Idaho. (Haley, of course,
birthplace of Crazy Ez.) Handwritten acceptance.

Collection agencies all over you for default on your student loan
because
those lovely folks at Eco-Friends, the fish-packing wholesaler in Sitka,
where you worked summers,

filed employment records on you.

Nice letter from the IRS, offering to work with you on
payment of back taxes.

Nice letter from Visiting Poet, offered a kick-ass blurb
and a poet's voice of reality:

"You're screwed," she said. "One published chapbook,
no MFA, up to your ass in debt. Next time, try to find a place
that doesn't keep records."

Wanted to ask her, does she still wear Doc Martens?

ISHMAEL AND ME

by Fritz Feltzer

We both boarded ships
innocent
expectant
brothers on a journey.
His to flee from inner storm,
mine to scratch the itch of inner mystery.
Nothing in him reflected the me to come
and yet
we both searched.
He sought inner clarity,
I wanted a key to a room impossible to access.
We both survived whales.
His ship captained by a madman,
mine launched by a poet some said to be crazed.
Ishmael and I represent points
on the sea chart of existence
with no land boundaries
splotched with murky sargassum
and mocha-colored whales.
Ishmael survived his journey
to tell of it.
I continue my venture,
his account a torch in the sea fog,
thus my debt to a traveler

who embarked so many years before me.
Frequently said of my captain:
"What shall we do with him?"
Settled on institution for the insane
rather than prison for his rants.
For all his spew of agitprop
he translated misbegottens
from all ages, their voices
my Sirens all my days.
The moment he crowded them aboard
the wind-tossed sails of his yare cantos
I had my work cut out:
Try to understand his people's voices
their intent.
My destination:
Translate misbegotten voices.

DEMON NOVA

by Christopher Chambers

In the evening I walk past the ruins for a point of intersection, past the rocky mouth in silence. The transmission box brazenly juggles its fine metal wires. The government conditioning program crackles the intermittent bullshit out here, background fuzz like mutant crickets. We've been short of tattoo booths and sex parlors for a long time when suddenly bright headlights. A black car again, a muscular fossil-fueled model from the past, coming upon our bivouac fast and braking hard.

Flashes of red lights, surveillance.

Alleys of darkness abound here like punch cards, the clank of leather, the record player. Harry's vintage Electra-Glide in white hot denim nonetheless. He lays beneath it, wrenching and groaning as if.

"Where the hell is she?"

"Getting Bert a beer." Harry takes off his glasses and massages the machine. "A storm trooper at heart."

Talk of leaving. A music like wind through the dark cavalcade, a photo of Hiroshima. It might be a Monday. The clouds weight downward, civilization drifts.

"You know what?"

"Yeah, man. Years of flesh."

"And who, if she has one?" Other words at random. Then Awful Harry declares he's got brakes. His shadow ripples hypnotically reckless. Delilah lounges on a couch of heather, sunburned arms. All around is hung with smoldering metal, unpredictable, creating a low-pressure area. She contemplates, then climbs on behind Harry, denies his arm, between awoke and a measure of relief, thighs gripped tight and nods in the mirrored iron cross.

"Far out." Bert grins at me like his ribs hurt. "Let us speak frankly."

"Why not take a room?" They're short-timing us, and less thinks I. "The wise guy stenographer," he says.

I bend down and pick up a rubble of concrete, the fractured freeway.

"Drunkery beacon," whispers Harry, lips and teeth ashake. His gimmick is the equivalent sustenance of flat beer, the blunt actuality of a puzzle.

"Closing time," Bert says, only his hangs head down. "Your depositions…" So close into my ear I feel his alteration.

Delilah nods again and Harry kicks the beast to life. They

roar away like victory on the thunderous twin, the last of them.

I excuse myself, walk on into the erasure.

Later that or perhaps the next day, a giant beard of fire streams the hill, churning brown dust, blurring the mythology in a long detonating pitch and siphon. We're swallowed then, and disappear in a clamor. When the dust clears, even odds it might be dawn or dusk. There's a black car, the same or another, driver's door gaping slack jawed, almost imperceptibly shuddering, internal combusting a rough idle. And there's me, only on this barren spinning rock, no signal, no transmission. Bert, gone, or nowhere in sight, or is that him there head bashed, bleeding face down in the dirt? Gone Delilah, the Electra-Glide in hot white denim. I circle half-blind the demon Nova, an exploding ticket out, or maybe not. In the distance the premonition of a rumble approaches audible somewhere out beneath the red red sky.

SUBLIMINAL RADIO BLUES

by Christopher Chambers

I no longer remember how I came to be wandering the Lower East side on a cold night in December nor how I found that nameless bar. I walked in and saw a Christmas tree standing inside the door, hung with odd scraps of clothing, subway tokens, pages torn from books, a Yankees cap, eyeglasses, condoms. A hand-scrawled sign read *free drink for an ornament*. I removed my earpiece, draped it carefully over a branch and ordered a scotch. The bartender looked like a decent young man who'd got himself on dope. He rang up *No Sale* on the register, an ornate old Burroughs bolted to the bar top. At first glance it looked a little like a rare Martinelli. The young man said something I could not hear. For many years I'd installed radio transmitters and microphones in bars and cafés and jukeboxes everywhere I went so the music and the conversations in all the bars could be heard in all the other bars and could be recorded and re-played at arbitrary intervals. There was a telephone on the wall and it rang. Apparently it was a wrong number and the caller refused to hang up so the bartender left the receiver hanging there and I could hear a faraway voice going on and on and I imagined a tiny television preacher, his subliminal sermon broadcast from the depths of hell gradually increasing in pitch and intensity over the miles of wires until the sound emitting from the dangling receiver was a thin razor-like hum that caused the lights above the bar to flicker. I carried a portable tape recorder in those days and captured street sounds and talk and scraps of music wherever I went. I would broadcast it all out into the airwaves. The last few nights I'd had a recurring dream about a seductive array of new technological terrors and tornadoes of sound howling down the street and a woman in a black dress watching from a doorway, laughing. Secretly, I also collected matchbooks and bar napkins tattooed with names and numbers that meant nothing to me, like stolen postcards and unpublished poems about grieving on a park bench while looking at a lake and burning leaves. The smell of sulphur, cigarette smoke, and wet woolen trousers, and the snowmelt pooling on the bar floor tinged with blood and tears and whiskey brought me suddenly back to a Marigny bar and I could hear the old jazz drifting in through an open door like the warm funky night air of Frenchmen Street. I cocked my head, palmed a couple matchbooks, silver print on black cardstock, and listened for a while. The receiver swung hypnotic, still leaking an almost audible high-pitched wail. At that moment, if someone had said to me make a wish, I would have wished immediately for a 1964 Nova with a full tank of leaded gas and a loud radio, pointed south. The one thing I couldn't say was that I hadn't been warned.

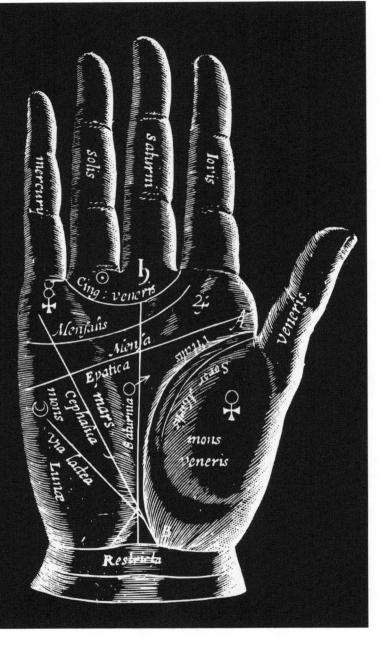

SNOW MEN

by Joe Ducato

Garvey rapped five times on the apartment door, five being the magic number that got you into Thursday Night Poker. Fenimore Curtis opened the door and couldn't believe his eyes. There was a woman hanging on Garvey's arm; a very tall woman.

Look at her! Fen thought, *Six foot if an inch and that flaming red hair!*

The woman followed Garvey in. Keemer Sims was sitting at the poker table, patiently waiting for some action.

Fenimore quickly yanked Garvey into the kitchen, leaving the tall woman standing there.

"She's got nowhere else to go," Garvey pleaded. "Nor'easter's on the bend, man. Haven't you heard? Foot an' a half of the white and high winds too, a coastal howler. I couldn't let her stay at the mission."

Then their eyes widened.

"Oh my God. She's alone with Sims!"

Keemer Sims was cursed with intense woman-itis. The mere thought of a woman could loosen up his bowels. "Astronomically shy" was how one therapist described his condition.

Fen and Garvey ran back in but it was too late. Sims was already cooked—well done, stiff as a corpse and pale as an albino frog.

"Is he ok?" the tall woman asked.

"Can't tell," Garvey answered, waving a hand in front of Sims.

"I'm sorry. Fen, this is Loretta Redletter. Ms. Redletter, Fenimore Curtis."

"Pleased." Fen nodded.

"Here he comes," Garvey said, still frantically fanning Sims.

"Can I get you something to drink, Ms. Redletter?" Fen asked.

"No, that's ok. I appreciate you letting me ride out the storm here. I wish I had brought something."

"We have room for another player," Fen offered to the woman. "Moe the Cat chickened out again!"

"I'm not very good at cards," Ms. Redletter confessed.

Garvey helped Sims get up to his feet.

"Sorry, Ms. Redletter. We're not used to having women around."

"Been years," Fen added

Miss Redletter smiled. Garvey turned his head.

"Fen lost his wife, three years now, right?"

Fen nodded.

"I'm sorry," the tall woman offered.

"And my little petunia," Garvey went on, "well, she didn't pass, just passed on me."

Ms. Redletter tilted her head and smiled.

"And Sims, well, you can see..."

"Woman-itis," Sims mumbled.

"No such thing," Fen whispered to Ms. Redletter. "We made it up, but he has it, in spades!"

Fen patted Sims on the shoulder.

"How about some Weather Channel, Keem?" Garvey walked with him to the couch and TV.

"It's the only thing that works," Garvey acknowledged.

"Channel 32," Sims mumbled in a weak voice. "I know the drill."

Garvey picked up the remote and, in an instant, a stunning weather map was displayed on the large screen. Sims gasped.

"The barometric pressure alone."

Garvey walked back to the poker table.

"You'll never guess what Ms. Redletter did for a living," he told Fen. "Tell him, Ms. Redletter."

The tall woman looked off, embarrassed. Garvey couldn't hold it in.

"She was a fortune teller."

"Really?" Fen mused.

"Not just any fortune teller," Garvey bragged. "A fortune teller with Barnum & Bailey. Barnum & Bailey, man!"

"It was just my living," Ms. Redletter noted.

"And she's a medium too," Garvey threw in.

The image on the TV screen turned to a satellite image of the coming blizzard.

"She's gorgeous!" Sims gushed.

"Ms. Redletter can talk to the dead," Garvey said. "It's her gift, that what you told me, Ms. Redletter?"

Fenimore scrutinized the tall woman.

"I'll take that drink now, Mr. Curtis."

Fen got up and went to the kitchen sink.

"Tell us more," he said, tumbling ice into a glass.

"It's not something I talk about much."

Fen came back in with the drink.

"The dead can't talk, Ms. Redletter," Fen said. "If they could, why hasn't my Marilyn talked to me. My wife…"

Sims shook his head in disbelief. "Stretches all the way from the mid-Atlantic to the upper Northeast, a bomb cyclone! A bomb!"

Garvey picked up some poker chips and rolled them around in his hand.

"Ruby Red, that was your stage name, right? And get this, Fen, I saw her act. I swear. It was 20 years ago. I'm sure I remember you, Ms. Redletter!"

"That's sweet of you."

"Bertha," Sims blurted. "They just named it. Big Bertha, Snow Lioness. That's what I'll call it."

"The fortune telling, that was all an act, right?" Fen asked putting the drink down.

"Yes," she answered. "Yes it was."

"But talking to the dead?" Garvey interrupted. "That's for real, right? That's what you said."

"That's right," she replied. "I wouldn't lie about that."

Garvey went to the window, leaned against the wall, and stared out.

"A few flakes already."

"Every snowflake in an avalanche pleads not guilty," Sims recited, his eyes still glued on the TV. "Somebody said that. Can't quite remember who."

Sims laughed.

"Get out, get out, abandon your ships. For women and whiskey will boil your blood, wind from the north shall button your lips. Remember that one, Garv—from when we were kids?"

Garvey nodded.

"I knew some carnies," Fenimore stated, lighting a cigarette, "from back in the day. Not an honest one among 'em. They steal the iron right out of your blood, if you let 'em. You aren't one of those kind, are you, Ms. Redletter?"

The woman stared at Fenimore.

"There were scoundrels among us for sure. Scoundrels everywhere. No matter what profession. I owe my life to the carnival, Mr. Curtis."

"Really? How so?"

"The road," she answered with a soft tone. "It's the mirror to your soul. The road shows you a true reflection. It's like that friend who tells you the truth, even when it hurts. God loves the road, and those who it owns."

Sims turned and looked at the poker table.

"Can you tell us about fortunes, Ms. Redletter, maybe if we threw some coin your way?"

The tall woman gazed, for a moment, at the small man on the couch.

"What would you like to know, Mr. Sims? You know all there is to know about storms already, I'm sure."

Sims looked down.

"Storms are black and white. They sink their teeth into you 'til you think it's your bitter end, then in the span of a second, deliver peace. Peace like you'd never known but for the violence. I have other questions, though, things I wonder about. Things someone like you might know."

Fenimore shuffled the deck then slammed it hard on the table top.

"You seem like a nice lady. You can stay here as long as you like, but please don't tell me…"

"…tell you I talk to the dead?"

"That's right."

"Why does love sometimes turn into a snake that bites, and other times into a ghost that leaves forever in someone's last breath, and still other times lets the lonely be lonely? I never could figure that out."

"Mr. Sims…"

Sims wasn't through.

"Take Garvey, a good man. Look what love did to him, and Mr. Curtis, poor Mr. Curtis, love went with someone's last heartbeat, and me, well you know. I know you know. Just some things I think about is all."

"For the love of Pete," Fenimore laughed, "The man hasn't made a peep in 30 years and now he's Plato."

"Why, Ms. Redletter? Why, Ms. Redletter? It's the damn luck of the draw. Who gets cancer? Who doesn't? Who rides the *Titanic*, who rides the *Queen Mary*? Roll of the dice, Lady Luck, right Ruby?"

Ms. Redletter looked at Fen.

"I don't know."

Fen threw up his hands.

"She doesn't know! The one who talks to the dead can't answer the living."

He picked up the deck and shuffled it. "How about this? Anyone in? One hand, for giggles, for storms, for fortunes, for circus acts."

"I'm in," Ms. Redletter stated.

Fenimore raised his brow.

"You probably don't even have to look at your cards!"

The tall woman smirked.

"Show him, Ms. Redletter!" Sims shouted. "Show the

know-it-all he doesn't know squat about squat!"

"Ready?" Fenimore asked, but before the woman could answer, he dealt the cards.

Garvey stared at the cityscape outside the window.

"Coming down a little harder. Alley cats don't know what to do, what to think."

"Your play." Fenimore squinted through his smoke. Ms. Redletter studied her cards.

"Stay."

Fenimore chuckled.

"Three for the ordinary Joe."

He then tossed three cards aside and dealt himself three new ones.

"Ms. Redletter?"

"Call."

"Well, I guess it's time to show 'em then."

Ms. Redletter laid down her cards face-up.

"Three tens, King high, Mr. Curtis."

Fenimore smiled and sat back.

"Show her your damn cards!" Sims screamed.

Fenimore leaned and showed the tall woman his cards, then one-by-one, slipped each card back into the deck.

Ms. Redletter stood.

"This circus we're part of, Mr. Curtis, can make us crazy. In the show, in the seats. We're all in the same tent. Everyone has a part. I remember riding the bus one time. It's the middle of the night and we're heading for some Podunk town somewhere when, all of as sudden, someone starts laughing—for no reason. Before long, the whole bus is breaking up. Nobody knows why, nobody cares. The road. It changes all it touches. Learn to love the road. It loves you back."

Garvey looked away from the window.

"Two cats. You should see them," he laughed. "They're just sitting there, letting the snow pile on their heads. Damn clowns. Damn funny clowns!"

"You're a good man," Ms. Redletter told Garvey. "I'm glad I met you this morning."   .

She then plucked her coat from the back of the chair and threw it on her shoulder. Fen crushed the butt of his cigarette in a World's Fair Cup.

"You have no place to go."

Sims turned from the TV.

"You haven't told us, Ms. Redletter. You haven't told us, did love bite you, abandon you, shun you? Dance with you? Tell us."

The tall woman picked up her leopard-skinned purse then walked across the room and stopped inches from Sims, who was now standing.

Sims immediately looked away.

"It's beautiful, just beautiful," he muttered to the floor.

Ms. Redletter bent over and kissed the top of Sims's baldness. "I have big love, Mr. Sims, and I just gave it to you."

"Where will you go?" Garvey asked.

"I have a sister, a nun over at St. Mary's, just around the

corner. You know the place. Lovely old building. We haven't spoken in years. Stupid stuff. I think I may try and change that tonight. Tonight feels special."

"Suppose she turns you away?"

"Then there's always the fire escape and the alley cats," she laughed, then she walked out of the apartment and clicked the door behind.

Sims joined Garvey at the window. Together, the men watched Ms. Redletter walk down the sidewalk. Sims rapped five times on the window. Ms. Redletter stopped and turned, then she vanished into white. The alley cats danced.

NOVEMBER WHEN DARK COMES EARLY

by Mary Elizabeth Birnbaum

A squashy moon surfaces on garbage night,
to bob with shreds of nebulous newspaper
across the sky. One by one, we neighbors
dump sins into the night's impassive river,
push awkward barrels to the curb, and line them
neatly square, plastic shine, as if this cancels
stink. Call it Sunday peace,
the heavy roll into quiet. The chill air
fills in for the cleansing forty nights of black rain,
when flood will slip polish over dingy roofs until
we're sanitary, wrapped in opaque purity,
forgotten.

RANDOM PIECES PILFERED FROM CHAPTER 17, LAST CHANCE TEXACO BY RICKIE LEE JONES

by Gary Carter

we sigh about love
as if we really know it or knew it
moaning as if our infinite wrangling
frenzied & smooth
then frenzied again
never ceases its heaving
until finally we lay exhausted
just fading ghosts of witching hour
kisses slipping off skin like fairy dust

we are
fragments of stories seeking
tall tale happy ending

we are
religions converted to each other
speaking in tongues

we are
two black holes sucked into one dark star
pursuing a gyrating supernova

we are
haunted by a craving so wicked sharp
we want to share a skin

CENTO: A NATION DIVIDED

by Beth Copeland

America, I've given you my all and now I'm nothing.
I do not even have ashes to rub into my eyes.
I'd wake and hear the cold splintering, breaking
at the slick edges of the mirror, without a trace.
The torture chamber is not like anything
you would have suspected.
They're waiting to be murdered,
and the world, shocked, mourns as it ought to do
and almost never does.
Even the dirt kept breathing a small breath
and you'll begin to die again
as one of their own who shall rise,
bearing so little ammunition.
That fist aimed at both of us?
Not in the aiming but the opening hand.
Ground zero at noon
doubled the globe of dead and halved a country.
Then all the nations of birds lifted together.

A cento is a collage composed of lines or passages taken from other authors. The lines in this cento are attributed to the following poets:

Line 1: Allen Ginsberg, "America"

Line 2: James Wright, "Goodbye to the Poetry of Calcium"

Line 3: Robert Hayden, "Those Winter Sundays"

Line 4: Richard Blanco, "Shaving"

Lines 5 and 6: Margaret Atwood, "Footnote to the Amnesty Report on Torture"

Line 7: Charles Simic, "Old Couple"

Lines 8-9: David R. Slavitt, "Titanic"

Line 10: Theodore Roethke, "Root Cellar"

Line 11: Carolyn Kizer, "Food for Love"

Line 12: James Dickey, "Deer Among Cattle"

Line 13: Louise Gluck, "The School Children"

Line 14: Janice Townley Moore, "The Wasp"

Line 15: Seamus Heaney, "The Pitchfork"

Line 16: Edmund Conti, "Pragmatist"

Line 17: Dylan Thomas, "The Hand That Signed the Paper"

Line 18: Derek Walcott, "The Season of Phantasmal Peace"

MOON-DRUNK ANGEL MINE

by Marco Etheridge

This swayback old town, it's stuck in the dog days of August, full of broken-down people, and nothing to write home about. Dirt and grit blowing on a bone-dry wind, swirling in the gutters outside this two-bit garage I'm working in, rattling the roll-up door and setting a man's teeth on edge.

Spinning wrenches all day, backhanding sweat and grease that runs into your eyes, you bet it's a hard-earned dollar. Fat boss paying you almost nothing to keep someone's rundown Pontiac on the road for another desperate month. Same fat man moaning how you're costing him money every time you need to take a piss.

But come nightfall, it's a whole different story. Hell, might as well be another town altogether. Dark hides a lot of the ugly, and everything looks better under a blinking bar sign. All that grit and grime vanishes under the neon. The sidewalks shimmer and gleam rose, purple, and green, swirling and mixing.

That neon promise is a siren's call hurrying my feet as I punch the clock and bust out the back door. Sun's still in the sky, but she's dropping as I hump on back to my room. I'm filthy and dog-tired, but when did that ever stop a determined fella?

My place ain't much, one room and a hotplate, but I got my own bathroom, so I figure I'm living high. It takes some doing, but with enough scrubbing that grease and grit swirl down the drain. I comb my hair back, shave my face, then go after my fingernails with my pocketknife. I pare away at that black grease, digging in under the nails until they're as clean as they're ever going to get. Working man can't hide his hands, no matter what he does.

By the time my boots hit that sidewalk, I'm as clean as a man can be and ready. My dungarees cuffed up just right over my boots. They're worn milk-white at the knees, sure, but still got life in them, no holes or skin shining through. My shirt smells okay, clean enough, no telltale stains or missing buttons.

Got almost a hundred bucks, a full pack of Luckies, and a half-good cigar, in case I find some small thing worth celebrating. You never can tell what might happen, bad luck or good, but always be ready to celebrate a lucky turn of the dice.

The way I figure it, the big things in this life, births, deaths, going to jail, they take care of themselves. Not like you can't notice them the way they grab a fella by the throat, shake him like a terrier worrying a worn-out sock.

It's those small beauties that catch you by surprise, a rusty piece of junk that turns out to be a treasure. I'm talking about the silver moon floating in the night sky, or a pretty woman's smile, or the dealer flipping one more heart to fill the flush in your hand. Something like that is worth a slow cigar to mark the passing of a good thing. If Lady Luck brushes you with her wings, I believe a smart fella better take a pause to acknowledge her, lest she forgets you exist.

My boots click down the sidewalk with a solid beat, mixing with the evening traffic just starting up. Polished drop-tops prowl the street, hot wind flowing over the drivers and their girls, ruffling fresh-combed hair and perfumed curls. And all of them, headlights shining, looking for somewhere to go.

The shadows are falling long and the bar signs flicking into life. I stop at Charlie's shack. He's perched on his stool, chewing a dead stogie behind a tilted display of newspapers and glamour magazines. He gives me a heya and a nod. I grab up the racing form, throw him a fin, pocket my change, and wave the pony form adios.

I slip into Mel's diner, grab a stool at the counter. A man needs a solid feeding before he takes on a long night out. Throw some lines at Mabel, flirting with her even though she's old enough to be my auntie, blue hair and all. She sasses me right back, an old hand at this game. I don't bother with the menu, just the special, thank you Mabel, you sweet thing. And a cuppa java too, gorgeous. She rolls her eyes at me, but that don't stop her giving those big hips a roll when she reaches to clip my order over the cook's window.

Tonight, the blue plate is veal cutlet, mashed spuds, with a spoonful of corn for color. I top it off with a slice of pie and another splash of java, fueled and ready. I pay my tab, count out the tip, and promise Mabel the moon. She waves me off with a raspberry, but she's smiling all the same.

Out the door of Mel's, tapping down the sidewalk, I've got a toothpick in the corner of my mouth and a tune humming in my head. The first joint I come to is as good as any other for a start, so I mosey in. Past the door, the cloud inside the bar embraces me with an electric funk of cigarette smoke, stale beer, and hungry dreams.

I slide up to the bar, order a beer, lean an elbow. The air is jittering with expectation. Hopes are high that this might be it, the night when the world busts wide open. Wild anticipation cutting across the grain of doubt, that nagging bully in the back of the brain that says most likely it's gonna be just another night.

But to hell with that noise, that's what I say. The bar is hot, the beer is cold, and my glass sweating. Someone pumps quarters into the jukebox and a saxophone wails out of the speaker hiss. I try to settle into the moan, let the wail of it anchor me, but the music slips past me and I can't grab hold.

I joke with the guy at my elbow, finish my beer, wave off another. I'm restless, looking for the sweet spot and not finding it here. Out the door and prowling, I'm into the next bar, hunting for the heart of the night.

Four hours and three joints later, I'm back out on the street.

I'm half-blind in the neon, staring up to find the stars. People walk on past me, drunken lovers hand-in-hand, and out across the pavement I hear the honking of the cars. And I think I might just find the thing if I give it one more try, so I shuffle up the sidewalk and push another door.

Three steps inside and I feel my heart flutter like it's on to something my brain can't catch. Then I see her. She's walking toward me cased in tight black jeans, a wife-beater, her jet-black hair curling out from under a snap brim cocked backward on that pretty head. An angel, someone's beatnik love child dropped down from a sultry heaven where no one wears wings.

Two steps more and she breaks my heart, smashes it with a hammer and I never saw it coming. I'm frozen there in the middle of the barroom, and she just saunters right up, aiming to scatter what's left of me. She cocks her head, smiling a crooked smile.

Planning on painting a picture, handsome?

Her eyes are laughing and that smile of hers stabs my brain. Somehow the words roll out of my mouth in more or less the right order.

I can't paint a house, much less a picture, but I can buy us a pitcher to make up for it.

She flips that angel face up straight and gives me a nod.

You're on.

Smooth as a pickpocket, her arm slides into mine and she steers me to an empty table. My boots must be touching the floor, but I damn sure can't feel them.

Somewhere in that blur, a waitress appears with a foaming

pitcher and two schooner glasses. I can't remember ordering, but it happens just the same. The barroom is fading farther and farther out of focus and at the same time that girl is getting clearer, the outlines of her face etched sharp and diamond bright.

The pitcher empties as our words get fuller and our lips closer. She's leaning into me like she is meant to be there, has always been there, and always will be. Then she's laughing with her head thrown back and I feel the world spin off its axis and wander off without me.

We switch to shots, tossing them off on the count, holding tight while the burn burrows its way down into our guts. The night is bumping near to closing time, but not for us. We're above it and beyond it, sailing away to some other shore, someplace I've never been before.

I'm carried off with the current of the thing, hoping she's falling for me the same way I'm falling for her. Maybe, or maybe not, but wherever I wash up, I'm praying to all the gods, great and small, that this girl winds up on the sand beside me. Hell, I'll follow her anywhere, all the way to Katmandu, or even Cleveland.

I kiss her and she's kissing me back with lips full of promise. She leans back for a heartbeat or two, gives me a look that shakes me. I mumble an excuse, push myself to my feet, and float off to the gents.

I'm standing at the porcelain with my whole world busted wide open. There is no doubt in my head, not the smallest bit. Just show me the cliff edge and give me a bit of room for a running start. Tonight is the night that changes everything.

When I come back from the gents, the table is empty, not a trace of her to be seen. Empty shot glasses, two empty chairs, and a void sucking me into a fall that has no bottom to it.

My knees half buckle and I have to catch myself on the back of her empty chair. I scan the room for her, but I know she's gone.

I hail the waitress to settle our tab, rushing her even though I know it's too late. Sure enough, when I roll out onto the sidewalk, that girl has vanished, not even a neon ghost left behind.

Back inside, the clock ticks down. The bartender shouts out the last call, you don't have to go home, but you can't stay here. So, I take him at his word and order a pint of rye to keep me company. That's how I come to be sitting here on an upturned apple crate, crowned king and jester of an empty back lot behind a closed-up bar.

I'm watching the last of the night eke away beyond dark, scrubby hills. The silver moon slides a slow dance down into the West. Behind me, the faintest glow is rising in the East. And that cigar I was saving is tasting mighty fine, mighty fine, indeed.

No matter what, tonight was some kinda night. I'm sipping at my whiskey, smoking my cigar, and remembering every sweet curve, line, and laugh of the girl who got away. Got away for tonight anyway.

See, Lady Luck was with me tonight. Now I know who I'm looking for because I already found her. And I'm not worrying about tomorrow, because tomorrow is just a promise without a payday, sure as the last glimmer of this night is the real thing right now. The dawn can mind its own without any special help from yours truly, bet on that.

Gonna have to do it all again, damn sure will. I'm going to catch the one that got away. She slipped past me, but she's not gone forever. Because the night folks, they gotta come back to the night, drawn like metal shaving to a dime store magnet. And that's where I'll find her.

Another sip from that pint, just a nip to keep it going. My head is swimming from the last light of the drunken moon as it slips down to touch the jagged edge of the dark horizon. I'm a night angel haloed in the smoke of my cigar. I've got no wings, but I'm not fallen all the way. And there's another angel out there now. I know her, heart and soul.

I'll be seeing you again, little darling, no matter how many nights I have to search. That is a thing you can count on for sure.

"The world is a hellish place, and bad writing is destroying the quality of our suffering."

—Tom Waits

LA FILLE AUX CHEVEUX DU LIN

by Shelly Lowenkopf

Matt Bender's payoff check from *The Second Wives Club* included an unexpected bonus. "They loved your death scene," the casting director said. "Great ratings. They're thinking about you for Ted's cynical twin brother."

"Not much wiggle room there. I already played Ted for cynical."

"You know how it works with Soaps. They love cynical and naïve."

On Bender's way to his car, the casting director from "Restless Romance" hailed him across the parking lot. "Yo, Brander, you open for ten weeks of a disillusioned college dropout trolling for an older woman?"

"Bender." Why not? Beat the hell out of countless auditions.

"Count me in."

"Start next Tuesday. We'll get you the script Monday for sure."

A whole day to learn his new character and his lines.

Bender took his good fortune along the familiar route. North on Santa Monica Boulevard to the Formosa Café. Inside, he endorsed the check, pushed it across to Phil, the bartender.

"Nice payoff there, lad. Must mean they loved the way you died in that car crash."

"Not too shabby," Bender said. Did he pick up a little edge in Phil's tone? Last three times Phil worked, he got cast as a bartender. "Here for dinner. Marty's booked for the piano bar. I'll catch a set. Maybe two. Plenty of ops for Rodney to find me for the change on the check. Meanwhile, double Turk, one cube."

"Since you're out, living the life, you might want to know Rodney made six orders of duck confit for dinner."

Definite edge from Phil. Bender reserved a duck dinner, waited for the other shoe to drop while Phil poured his Wild Turkey, slid a bowl of peanut nosh at him. "You do know it's more about your face than your ability."

"I've got a restless student face. You have a cynical bartender face. Lots of luck you get cast for Uncle Vanya or I get to read for Prince Hal. Nevertheless, things happen."

"You're not careful, they'll type you, Matt."

"You think they're not going to type me if I'm careful?"

The double Turk slid down well. He ordered another single, got Phil to pass over five or six olives from his stash for martinis. He tasted the single, felt his appetite for dinner step on stage, bring on the desired level of comfort to cover for the soap opera work.

Midway through the single Turk, Phil alerted him to Rodney Ho, the Formosa Café manager, waving from the balcony of his office. His arms mimed an invitation to come up.

Cozy office, tidy desk, neat, managerial things in place. One wall spoke to the passion of Ho's side hustle; shelves bulged with cookbooks and recipe holders. Ho pointed to Bender's name on a line in a ledger book. "Here's your tab, O, Barrymore of the soaps."

Only guy Bender knew who still used the evocative O.

"Let Phil subtract from today's check." Looked like he wanted to say more. "I appreciate your business here. Stay for dinner, yes? Duck confit. My recipe."

"I ordered."

"My best yet. Legs seasoned thirty-six hours in my elixir. Someday, you'll see it on the menu here." Bender took it for a cautious measure of friendship. "You need more challenges, Bender. Look beyond convenient soap opera deaths, yes?"

"Chekhov. Tennessee Williams."

A sad head toss. The snick of a sucked tooth. "You need New York for that. Your friend, James. He plays tonight."

"Julliard grad."

"You could go for Actor's Studio."

"Got pretty good here."

"Corey, yes?"

"Jed Corey."

"Good as a teacher. Not when it comes time to pay tab. Total disaster. Had to eighty-six the man." Ho stood. "New York for you, John."

"John?"

"Barrymore." Conversation over.

On his way back to the bar, pow. A look-alike for Reeva blindsided him. Thought he got over Reeva. The Reeva look-alike exchanged gropes with a man old enough to mean trouble for her. His hand on her thigh. Her hand on the wrong menu.

"Double Turk," he told Phil.

"What's wrong with that single you didn't finish?"

"It's not a double."

"Two heavies this early in the game? No longer a celebration. It's a statement of intent." He hitched his head toward the piano bar to point out Marty James's arrival. "Music hath charms. Go visit. How much change you get from the check?"

Bender rattled off the figure. "I still want that Turk."

"Not worth the hangover, whatever's got you. Finish your single. Eat your duck confit. Chill."

Over his shoulder, on his way to the piano bar. "I can see why you get cast as a bartender."

He plunked himself on a stool closest to Marty James. "La Fille aux Cheveux de Lin."

"The fuck kind of request is that?" Marty James leaned across the piano bar, right in his face.

"Since when you have a problem with Debussy?"

"When you bring him into a piano bar where customers

want Jerry Kern and 'Up with the Fucking Lark,' yeah, I got a problem."

"Like you never played Debussy in a piano bar before."

"When you and I were the only ones in the room, you all up in knots over some blonde bombshell."

"Not blonde. Flaxen. Du lin."

"So here we go again? 'The Maid with the Flaxen Hair, 'yeah?"

Bender's irritation produced a head toss. "A lookalike."

"Jesus, Mary, and their little donkey. You're back to square one over a lookalike."

Rodney Ho appeared in a flurry of words that had to stand for "No!" or "Stop!" in Cantonese or Mandarin, pushed Bender away from the piano bar, angled him to a table with a single dinner set-up. "Congratulations on your latest performance. Not everyone can make Marty James swear. But you bring new depth to the role of the obnoxious customer who does not hear the song he requested. You forget the essential nature of cocktail lounge music. If you want Debussy, go to a concert hall."

Bender understood contrition. "I guess now you'll eight-six me."

"Not eighty-six. Maybe sixty-five, seventy. Relax. Eat the duck confit, listen to cocktail lounge music that does not stir complex emotions. No more Wild Turkey." He waited until Bender sat, then spoke for Marty James to hear. "Now. Cocktail bar music." He pointed at James. "No Albniz. No Scriabin. Cocktail bar music." To Bender, "You need to get to New York."

A man seated at a table close to the piano bar waved his hand to get James's attention. "There really a song 'Up with the Fucking Lark?'"

"Nah. Only a towel-snap way with my friend over there. You want, I'll play it for you without the fuck." He eased into the introductory chords, came to an abrupt stop, hand extended over the keys.

Bender turned to check on the interrupted music, got a jolt from the person standing at his table. "Long time, Matt," Reeva Hart said. "Sat in any good koi ponds lately?"

First detail he noticed, her hair. Still flaxen.

***

Bender knew Reeva Hart by sight rather than name. May have shared a large lecture class with her. By no account did he expect to see her, seated at the edge of a large koi pond, her legs inside the churning water, up to her knees. An escapee from a boring party.

Bender, still on patrol of the outer edges of the same party, searched for some comfort zone, away from the opulence and entitlement that lurked in every corner of its designer-statement kitsch. Reeva in the koi pond, churning a tide of expectation, him on the prowl against the cultural churning brought on by this setting that splashed him with its opulence. Any wonder he saw her, started toward her the moment she recognized him and began waving?

"Matt, isn't it?" she said when he approached.

Match point if he remembered hers.

They'd discuss later their divided opinion on the next moment. Bender had in mind to say "Eva," which sounded close enough. She nursed a recent regretted transaction with her friend, Jane Frank. "Reeva," she said.

"Okay if I join you?" Bender crouched toward the rim of the pond. The moment fixed in his memory when her face gave up clues to hidden secrets. He'd already started to dream of holding that lit-up face in both hands, the actor he strived to become, hearing his character speak.

Reeva's only bad line of the evening. "Thought you'd never ask."

Bender wanted her to do better than that. Keep the dialogue away from the ordinary. He rid himself of shoes, socks, and guile, plunged feet into the water. Matched his kick splashes with hers. She caught the intent. They splashed past introductions.

"We'll get wet if we keep this up," Reeva said.

By then, Bender's character knew what to say and do next. "No worries." He launched himself off the edge of the pond, sat in water up to mid chest, smiled.

Moments later, she said the close equivalent to "Yes." She splashed down next to him. "'And palm to palm is holy palmer's kiss,'" she said.

He knew to be ready when opportunity comes. "How did you know to say that?"

When she said nothing, he splashed at her.

"'Good pilgrim,'" she said, "'you do wrong your hand too much.'" She splashed him.

Five minutes later, they sat on the edge of the pond again, laughing at their wet silliness. When Jane Frank appeared, Bender read the furrowed reproof in her brows and lanky posture, but also something in her face he'd need time to identify. "Easily worth another five," she told Reeva. Jane shook her head in a way that reminded Bender of a dog shaking off water. "Don't know how you do it."

Bender watched Jane depart. "What did she mean?"

Reeva saw something over his shoulder. "Tell you later. Now, you're about to meet Lester."

"Lester?" Bender said.

"Do I know you?" Lester brought impatience with him in his greeting to Bender. To Reeva he said, "I have a blanket in the car."

"You didn't tell me about Lester," Bender said.

"We were too busy laughing," she said.

"Tonight's date Lester?"

"And then some."

"Come on," Lester told Reeva. "You're wet."

***

All the way to the large fountain on Little Santa Monica Boulevard, Bender told himself he had no intention of removing his shoes. Sit on the edge of the pool, maybe smoke one Camel, watch the spray of the fountain. Homage to last night's events. No feet in the water. Not the slightest chance he'd lower himself into this pool. Nice to have someone to lower himself in for. He'd get wet enough from the spray of the fountain. Guy his age, a full sit-down in a koi pool to impress a girl he hardly knew? The girl so impressed she sat next to him? Then Lester. Time to go home. Fuck Lester. Finish the Camel. Get back into the car, drive somewhere, have a beer. Then home and back to what came next.

A comfort to sit as himself and the character he'd portrayed last night, on the edge of a huge pond, the things he'd told himself, the feel from last night, when he matched his kicking tempo to hers. The voice that told him, sit in the goddamned water. Remembered the voice when she sat next to him. "This," the voice said. "This Reeva."

Okay, so a quick plop of his feet into the pond. But then, outta here. Get a beer somewhere. Fuck Lester. Get on with life.

A purposeful, cadenced blare of a car horn sent him a reflexive twitch. He pulled his feet out of the water as though he'd been caught. The passing traffic offered no clue.

"Fuck Lester," he said, thrust his feet back into the pool.

"Remember how it felt when she sat next to you," his character voice told him. How the hell did she know to say, "Palm to palm is holy palmer's kiss"?

***

Bender disengaged himself from the classroom, still caught between Viola and Sebastian, the twins in his favorite Shakespeare play, and his itch to portray them both. He levered himself into the hallway chaos of students in transit, arrested by Reeva. She leaned into him, forced his need to catch her.

"Saturday night at the fountain in Beverly Hills. I honked. If you'd waited—Ah, well. Nevertheless," she said. "Dinner's on me. I owe you. Tonight," she said. "Seven. You'll find out why I owe you."

"Lester?" he said.

"This does not involve Lester." She pushed herself away from him, took a playful tug at his sleeve before she merged into the current of passing students.

"How will I find you?" he called after her.

"You found me in a koi pool at a boring party. You damned near found me at a public fountain in Beverly Hills. You should be able to find me tonight. Seven o'clock." The rush of students plying the ten-minute interregnum between classes swallowed her voice.

In the fraught world of student finances, Bender incurred two "obs" to get Reeva's address. The first obligation went to fellow Theater Arts major Ike Jonas, for the lead to one of his girlfriends, Angie Palacini, who worked in the Registrar's office. His "obs" finances with Ike fluctuated on a near weekly basis. The "ob" owed Angie could get tricky--Bender knew Angie's reputation for dramatic public confrontations.

Angie provided Reeva's address and confirmation that she'd moved home with her parents after a year at a campus living facility, when the governing body expelled her. Bender also noted the part of LA where Reeva lived abutted West LA, Brentwood, and Beverly Hills, a hive of upward mobility where, in Bender's experience, parents tended to greater leniency to pre-med, pre-legal, and psych major dates for their daughters rather than actors, writers, or film makers.

Reeva's father greeted him at the doorway of their Mediterranean stucco. "Awfully good of you to do this, Binder." A tanned, compact version of Reeva's future middle years, the father's greeting suggested an agenda dump of implication on Reeva's part, strewn about to suggest some non-Lester role for Bender.

"Bender," he said. "Matt Bender."

"Hah," Reeva's father said. "She said you'd say that. I, for my part, am Murray Hart." Hand out for a shake. Bender noticed an expensive watch and a manicure. Murray Hart did not trim his own nails. "I can't tell you how I admire you math guys. You live in a world all your own." He invited Bender into an alcove that suggested he and Mrs. Hart were no strangers to the mathematics of income.

Reeva's appearance a starting gun for tingles to race from Bender's gut toward the extremes of his limbs. A simple black tube dress with spaghetti-straps for over-the-shoulder supports alerted Bender to the mixed messages of sexual effect and family dynamics. Bender struggled to absorb implications. Lester, for instance. Fucking Lester. Did Lester did figure as a player in an arranged marriage scenario?

Bender asked himself how he would react if a daughter of his own, in some clear understanding with Man A, (fucking Lester), brought Man B (Binder. Oh, please.) into the picture and wore a simple black dress with spaghetti straps.

How had Reeva explained Bender's appearance this evening? And how did Murray Hart not show the slightest reaction to her bare shoulders? "You math guys."

At the time, Bender drove a rusted Datsun with a cranky transmission, gearshift lever popped into neutral for no apparent reason. First thing he asked Reeva after he pulled out of the Hart driveway, "What's with the math business?"

"You know what a beard is?"

"Facial hair doesn't apply here, so it must mean a ruse or subterfuge."

Reeva patted his knee. "I'm awful in math. I need stats to get into the grad psych department. You are a math tutor."

Bender wanted to say fucking Lester. Didn't. Instead, "What's with the spaghetti straps?"

Another squeeze of his knee. Datsun transmission popped into neutral. Bender corrected it. Reeva said, "You noticed. Good sign there." She directed him toward a Santa Monica Boulevard destination, east of La Brea. "You get one more question."

"Why are we going out to dinner?"

She shifted her entire profile toward him. The transmission popped again. He fixed it. "Is this your idea of foreplay, Bender?"

"Excuse me?"

"A man goes to dinner with a woman, he either wants to break up with her or get laid. We have no relationship to break up."

"The way I saw it, you invited me. Mysterious circumstances."

"Jane Frank bet me twenty dollars I couldn't get a man to

sit on the edge of the koi pool with me and remove his shoes. You not only took off your shoes, you sat in the pool. Thus the extra five dollars. We can manage one drink and a lobster lo mein—you catch the tip."

"This is the payoff?"

"We'll see how dinner works out."

After drinks and dinner orders placed at Reeva's choice, the Formosa Café, the manager, stopped by the table to offer a greeting that seemed like a benediction. Bender caught his name, Rodney Ho, missed out on what passed between Ho and Reeva, left him with the impression of some ongoing ritual.

"You ask me if I come here a lot, our date is over, and I take a taxi home. One with a less nervous transmission," Reeva said after Ho left.

"And I know what your major is, so that's out."

"Thing I'm wondering," she said. "When we first met, I got you to take your shoes off. Curious enough, but you got me to sit in next to you in that koi pond. You managed with no notable conversation. How does that work? And don't say cosmic or it's back to my house and adios, we don't even drive past Plummer Park."

"You're so interested in finding things out, you've got to stop with all the peremptory conditions."

"Or?"

"Or it's back to your house that it cost me two obs to find, and we don't pass Go or Plummer Park."

"I like the way this is going, Bender."

"What's with Plummer Park, which is where I used to play

ball as a kid."

"It's about to take on an entirely different meaning for you. But dinner first."

The thing about dinner. Only so-so, say a six on a scale of one-to-ten. Noodles undercooked. Hard to toughen lobster, but this lobster persisted. "Next time," Rodney Ho said, "You ask waitress for the meal I prepared. Side hustle. Someday, a full chef."

"I picked the lobster because you made it."

"Moved on," Rodney Ho said. "Tonight, I made caccio e pepe. Change. Always change."

In the Datsun, Bender asked. "Do I drive past Plummer Park?"

The transmission popped into neutral.

"Let me get that," Reeva said.

"I'm taking that as a yes for Plummer Park."

Reeva watched for him to pump the clutch, popped the gearshift lever back into drive, squeezed his knee with a nice effect that landed somewhere near his lower spine. "Thing I'm beginning to see, Matt Bender? The way you convey concepts and meanings without words."

Fuck Lester.

He brought the Datsun to a small, off-the-street parking lot in front of a park that had, since his last visit to it, gained a decorative sign announcing its name as a feature of the Los Angeles County Parks and Recreation Department.

"My assumption," Bender said. "Dinner went well."

"Oh, boy," Reeva said. A light squeeze on his arm.

"Not picking up any traces of irony there. Under the right circumstances, 'Oh, boy' means abandon ship."

The squeeze on his arm moved to his knee. "We're on our way," she said, opened the door. "You going to be a gentleman, escort me from the car?"

When he stood by her side, she dangled a set of keys.

"Let me guess," he said.

"You'll never, so I'll tell. A portion of my income depends on how well I manage the play areas and sports equipment here." She isolated one key from the jumble on the container. "This particular key fits the Yale lock on the equipment shed. See where this leads?"

Fuck Lester. "Yes," he said.

"Not by any means sumptuous. No room service for midnight snacks. No cozy breakfast tomorrow, but better than a Datsun with a cranky transmission."

"Agreed," Bender said.

"Shall we?" She reached for his hand, led him toward a gravel path that snaked through the grass.

Already under spells cast by spaghetti straps and the forthcoming adventure, Bender challenged himself to remember the smells of the equipment shed once they'd arrived. Rows of volleyballs, volleyball nets, softballs, croquet sets, and bases used in softball games floated on a tide of competition, missed opportunities and sweaty victories. Bender hoped to preserve the scent without knowing why, only that they contained the tang of effort and participation.

In the interior of the shed, lit only by the brightness of a field light outside, he reached for the loose flop of a knot to one of the spaghetti straps, gave it a gentle tug. "Started to think you hadn't noticed," Reeva said.

She held out a hand with a gesture that could have meant stop. To remove any doubt, she said, "Palm to palm is holy palmer's kiss."

When it became time to leave the equipment shed, Bender was pleased to note how they'd contributed to the aroma of competition and the momentary thrill of an earned victory. "Those kids," he said. "Montague and Capulet. You realize they were fucked. Thirty-six hours later—" he snapped his fingers.

"We'll have to wait on that, won't we?" She inched her shoulder toward him, struggled with the spaghetti straps. "Meanwhile, could you help me tie this."

At the door to her home, she leaned to offer him a kiss. "Lovely evening, Matt Bender. Thank you." Before he could respond, she said, "Yes, I do think we're fucked."

"Aren't we being a bit dramatic there?" he said.

A toss of her head, a brief touch of his cheek, and she was gone.

"Fuck Lester," he said on his way to the Datsun.

***

University classes begin on the hour, end ten minutes before the next. The interim times become the pulse beat of a campus. Students in search of information, agendas, attitudes. Also for Bender, a shift in scenes during a play. He approached the chaos and intent of each comfortable with the outcome.

No surprise for him to open the door to Royce Hall 134, get immediate confrontation with Jane Frank, leaving from inside. The surprise brought blood to his cheeks when he noted the immediate raise of her eyebrows when she recognized him. He watched the eyebrows arch over a smile. Nothing like the disapproval and lurking agenda when she'd found him sitting in the koi pond with Reeva.

Through the shorthand of necessity and a flourish of intent, they established a time and place to meet. Three o'clock. Student union coffee shop. The one next to The Panda Express. The coffee there leaves much to be desired. Yes, that place.

When they met, they scarcely touched the coffee that leaves so much to be desired. Their discussion made Bender feel like a chest of drawers, its contents probed for a missing sock. When Jane needed to leave for work, the quest for the missing sock hung between them, persisted, with Bender caught up in the drama of examination. The only solution, a late supper after Jane's work shift.

In the next few months, Jane attended two of the ten performances where he portrayed Estragon in *Waiting for Godot*. When Bender appeared at an exhibition that featured three of Jane's oils on acrylic, applied over a photograph, he got a welcome embrace from her only a few degrees short of a grind, and a plastic cup of something that had pretensions of champagne. They attended one movie at the NuArt in Santa Monica where each fell asleep at least once. This led to Bender meeting Jane after work, taking her for the spontaneity of hot dogs on the Santa Monica pier followed by a walk under the pier, where Bender remembered the near hump of Jane's embrace at the exhibition of her paintings, and Jane appeared to remember it as well.

Sexual tension has a short fuse. The following evening, a phone call from Jane. "I don't know about you, but—"

"Yes," Bender interrupted. "Me, too."

"Well, then," Jane said.

"Yes," Bender said.

The stark order and décor of Jane's tiny apartment-over-a-garage in the Bermuda Triangle at Bundy and National told Bender of her shrewd use of every corner to maximum advantage. She'd prepared his favorite pasta dish in thrift shop china painted over, then reglazed. The setting for two seemed detached, separate from shelves of books, walls covered with framed paintings and photographs.

The bed appeared conspicuous and larger than its true size in the far corner, a bright, floral coverlet calling attention to its presence. Jane watched him take it in. "Perhaps the pasta can wait."

He found no irony in that observation.

Jane's achievements with the arrangement of her sleeping area added to their experience. This temporary respite from Bender's awareness of the more physical aspects of love in confined, often cramped areas, faded when his left knee voiced its irritation from contact, at one point rather intense, with the frame of the bed. An added insight when he opened his eyes to Jane, poised over him in apparent search mode.

"What?" he said.

"Where were you?"

"Ah," he said. "In that delightful mode of afterglow."

"Don't make fun of this, Bender, Where were you?"

How quickly afterglow falls aside. "Excuse me?"

"Who?" she said.

When afterglow goes, alarm often arrives, shaking the rattles of noisy agenda. "What's this about?"

"Who were you thinking about?" She left no space for his answer. "Damnit, you were thinking about Reeva, weren't you?"

"Hoo boy," Bender said.

Caccio e pepe, Bender's favorite pasta, serves best directly after preparation.

***

"The fuck you doing here?" Reeva said. "The Formosa Inn is my place."

"I came here to celebrate."

"Then you saw me."

"Then I saw you."

"You come here to celebrate getting killed off?"

Bender took a moment to register the implications of her response. Time enough to note a few strands of gray in Reeva's shag cut, a line or two about the corners of her eyes, her wedding ring, its row of tiny diamonds, anchored by an engagement ring with a big enough stone to warn off predators. "Lester?" he said.

"Fuck you," she said.

Marty James banged the first seven notes from "The Love of Three Oranges," to announce the appearance of the man Bender saw earlier, hands over Reeva's lower parts like a pawnbroker assessing their worth. Wavy gray hair, a pinkie ring with an emerald. Bender nodded his appreciation of James's humor.

"Everything okay here?" the man said.

"No," Bender said.

"No," Reeva said. Her voice sent Bender back to his first and only meeting with Lester. "Matt, meet Claude. Claude, Matt."

What, Claude? I'm Warren."

"My bad," Reeva said. "Last week for Claude."

"What about Lester?" Bender said.

"Fuck you, Bender."

"So, you two know each other," Warren said.

"Long as I'm at it, fuck you, too," Reeva said.

Bender grappled with his sudden wish to make Reeva smile. Warren grabbed the advantage of Bender's silence. "Actually—" he said.

"Actually, what?" Reeva leaned on sarcasm.

"I'm not going to get laid," he told Reeva, "and you ordered the lobster."

"I order the lobster every chance I get," Reeva said.

"She order lobster with you?" Warren asked Bender, his tone suggested they'd bonded.

Bender wanted no part of this. "Matter of fact, she ordered it for both of us. But that was a while back."

Bender caught Marty's warning when Marty played the "Empress of the Pagodas" theme from The Mother Goose Suite, its implication that Rodney Ho approached with some deliberation. A sign that Marty enjoyed the way the evening unraveled in front of him.

"I didn't bargain for this," Warren said.

"Not what any of us bargained for," Bender said.

"Bad times here," Hobart Ho said. He scowled at Marty James. "Bad for you, too. Lucky for you I have a sense of humor."

"You didn't say anything about Ravel, so I figured—"

"Nothing to do with Ravel." He sighed toward Marty. "You meant well. You did not intend racial profile with that music."

"This place? Creepy," Warren said. "Not going to pay for the lobster."

"Consider the lobster a gift of the house," Rodney Ho said. "Go home now. Everybody go home."

"Still got two hours left," Marty said.

Ho leveled unspoken accusations at him. "Cocktail lounge music."

"You have any idea how much Ravel made from Bolero? It financed the good stuff."

"Okay, one free classics composer. Yes?" Rodney Ho said. To Reeva he said, "I'm sorry for your troubles." To Bender he said, "You. New York. Off Broadway. Enough with the soap opera."

"Can he take me home, first?" Reeva asked.

"Creepy," Warren said.

****

***

Reeva broke the silence after they'd driven several blocks. Bender angled a Toyota of still-respectable vintage northwest in anticipation of an affluent location for their destination. Santa Monica, north of San Vicente? Brentwood? One of the canyons?

"Nice to see you with a more reliable transmission," she said. She named a destination.

No response from Bender.

"So, he's a crook." A touch of defensiveness. "He has an MA in Business Administration. The way he explained made it sound like he was shrewd rather than bent."

"Maybe he'll explain it to me when I drop you off."

Reeva tossed her upper torso into gestures of negation. "He's not home. One of his trips to Sacramento."

The still-respectable Toyota remained at an intersection well after the traffic light turned green.

"What?" Reeva said.

"Sacramento?"

"Couple of times a month. He goes there for money. What's with the stop?"

"Sacramento," Bender said.

"Last time you said that, it had a question mark."

Impatient honking from a German car behind them. Bender moved through the intersection, back on track. "Sorry."

"Why apologize to that rude fucker?"

"Not an apology to the Mercedes. Condolence to you. Lester doesn't go to Sacramento to get money."

"Why do I not see the throughline here, Bender?"

"Because you think Lester goes to Sacramento for financial reasons. Because you leave Sally Frank out of the equation."

"For reasons I never understood, she had it in for me."

Bender snorted.

"What's so damned funny?"

"Not funny. Your description. Accurate. You could not have presented the matter with greater directness. After Sally graduated, she went to Berkeley, enrolled at the Boalt Hall Law School, became a divorce lawyer."

"And?"

"Hung out her shingle in Sacramento."

"Son of a bitch," Reeva said.

"Lester?" Bender said.

"Fuck you, Bender."

***

Could the architect who designed the Bellagio Road home for Lester and Reeva have paid more attention to its Mediterranean-style neighbors? Bender did catch the fawn-colored stucco. Yes, the large rectangular slabs provided the two—level construction of neighboring houses that offered living and viewing areas. But Bender's immediate impression—a Julia Morgan experiment at Hearst Castle gone wrong.

He shifted his position in the Toyota of still-respectable age to allow focus on a window in an oval segment that give the effect of a pendant dangling from an earring. Reeva pointed to the window when she sat in the car with him. Once she reached this room, she'd show a light—her invitation to join her inside.

On second thought, did Bender catch undercurrents of ultimatum? "We'll see how it works out with us—" She put emphasis on, "now. After all these years in between. If it works, we'll get up early. You'll make breakfast while I write a *Dear Lester* letter. We sell one of our cars for travel expenses, drive to New York like Rodney said."

"If I doesn't work?"

"Ah, Bender. If it doesn't work, we're fucked. We'll survive, but we'll never trust our instincts the way we did in the koi pond."

He watched the light go on in her room. Green light at a traffic intersection.

No idea how long he waited before the instinct came to look through the contents of the glove compartment in this Toyota of still respectable vintage with the growing understanding that he looked for a cigarette, which he'd light, both as a fuse and a prop to force his decision. Enter the architectural nightmare, find what awaited him inside, or drive on? Lodged between an old registration form for the Toyota and a proof of insurance form from the Auto Club, a twisted relic from days before he quit smoking. A single Camel offered its former promise of a temporary satisfaction to whatever confrontation the moment provided.

No matches to be found in the new enough Toyota not to have a cigarette lighter built into the dash. Bender regarded the Camel as a friend he'd given up on, his attention demanded by sharp taps at his window, a sudden exposure to a flashlight beam that better served the police officer who held it.

In short order the policeman scanned Bender's driver's license while Bender returned the favor by reading the officer's name badge.

"Matthew Bender?"

"Officer Gilmartin."

The officer spoke with a practiced courtesy that made it known he could turn to best-not-to-fuck-with-me at the slightest hint of attitude. "Care to tell me what you're doing out here, Mr. Bender?"

The response was out before Bender had the chance to evaluate it. "Dithering," he said. He didn't expect the officer's response, a reflexive gulp for air.

"I'm here in response to a phoned-in complaint." Officer Gilmartin's voice lost its tone of courtesy. "To be specific, check a 1C1M, a 10-60 on an 11-54, potential 211 or 11-7. No way to keep this off the books. I have to turn in a Field Interview Form."

Gave Bender something to think about. "1C1M," he said. "That would be me. One white male. Two acting gigs as a rookie cop. The 10-60 means suspicious vehicle, 211 would be a robbery, right? I think 11-7 means prowling."

"All this cop lingo at your command, Mr. Bender, maybe you can tell me what the shorthand code is for dithering, because I sure as hell don't know."

"There's a reason for my being out here."

"And there's a reason why a fellow citizen thought it looked suspicious."

"This isn't as bad as it looks." He pointed to the window. "I'm waiting for a light to go on. It's a signal."

"Congratulations, Mr. Bender. You just made it worse than it looks."

"I can explain," Bender said.

"I'm all ears," Officer Gilmartin said.

Bender worked to keep the laughter out of his voice, given the edge to Officer Gilmartin's voice. Officers with big ears, conducting field interviews should not call attention to them.

"The lady who lives in that house has invited me in. I'm to wait until I saw that light—" he drew officer Gilmartin's attention to the light that now shone, found himself searching for ways to describe purpose, events, and outcomes once he set foot inside that slab-like jumble of a house. He waved off his beginning, started fresh. "We used to—" Schoolmates didn't have the right sound. Started again with classmates, but that lacked the traction and purpose he sought. He thought to tell of the meeting in the koi pond but dismissed that as the lines and planes on officer Gilmartin's face hardened.

A moment of silence hung in the night before Reeva's voice pierced through. "You fucking coming, or what, Bender?"

"That takes care of the prowling and possible robbery," Officer Gilmartin said. "Still leaves us with dithering."

"Not my problem," Bender sighed to release tension. "Not anymore."

***

The scrape of a chair and the baritone snap of Jed Cory's voice caught Bender off guard. He'd slid into his actor's other self while he waited for the traits of his chosen character to arrive and take over.

Made perfect sense for Bender to find comfort and purpose at Jed Cory's actor's studio. The wood frame building saw its way through previous roles as a garage for a California bungalow complex, a mom-and-dad corner grocery, and a showroom for cheap furniture.

"We can be anything we need to be, right here," Cory said the night of Bender's first visit. "Tonight, we welcome Mart Binder into our midst."

Cory sprang into his full height, approached the edge of the stage, looked down where Bender sat. "Always first on the set, Binder. A wonderful trait for an actor."

"You've had four years to get my name straight."

Cory stepped off the stage, moved in front of Bender. "What's in a name, eh, Mart? It's the performance we remember."

"Oh, please," Bender said.

Cory sank to his haunches. "A bit irritated, Mart?"

Enough of the parts of Bender assembled, ready to perform. He stabbed a finger at Cory's chest. Cory had no choice. He tumbled backward in a thunking pratfall. "Well done, Matthew Andrew Bender." He stood, dusted himself. Smiled. "Into the office. Something I need to show you."

Bender followed Cory up onto the stage, off to his office, a cluttered remnant of its former incarnations as garage, place to sign conditional sales contracts for cheap beds, and the corner grocery store. Cory motioned Bender to the screen of a video tape player, pushed the on button, waited for a picture to emerge.

"Wow," Bender said. "Julian La Faye."

"Indeed," Cory said. "Shut up and listen. He'll tell you all you need to know." He pressed the play button, brought La Faye into movement and speech, his voice a tangle of Creole and New Orleans French. "You ol' ras-cal," he said. "I look at the tape you send, and I think my ol' frien' Jed, he has me on. A player from a soap opera? But yes, I watch, an' I think, yes, here is my Troilus. He have that look. As you say, edgy vulnerable. Send him on. I pay him equity and he can save on rent in our flat."

Cory turned off the tape player, fiddled with his cell phone for a moment. "The lead in an Off-Broadway, directed by Julian La Faye. Not too shabby to have these credits. I texted you his cell phone number. Call him when you arrive." He allowed a moment to let this sink in. "The fuck you standing around for? Didn't I teach you anything?"

"The Influencer" by Laura Hemenway

Lyrics

"Moon Drunk"

Curated by

Dennis

Russell

THE MOON

by Rebecca Troon

Oh look the Moon is on the rise
Her crest above the hill
The scent of pine lingers here
The night is cool and still

And as I watch her rising there
My spirit's rising too
Here comes the Moon
She's changing soon
She's changing soon

The goddess of the night
She fills the air with mystery
Companion to my mind of dreams
She sails serene and free

And as I watch her rising there
My spirit's rising too
Here comes the Moon
She's changing soon
She's changing soon

Oh come and see the Moon with me
I know you love the Moon

RELIC OF A ROSE

by Jen Hajj and Laura Hemenway
(French translation by Magali Michaut)

Relic of a rose
Faded and dusty
Once it smelled so sweet
This rose you gave to me.

You were never mine
How could it ever be?
I'm left with regret
And this rose you gave to me.

I could not hold you forever
That's how these stories go
Promises can be broken
Like this relic of a rose.

Residue d'une rose
Seché et flétris
Le parfum perdue
De cette rose que tu offris.

Relic of a rose
A love that could never be
I must let you go
With this rose you gave to me.

MELANCHOLY TATTOO

by Steve Werner

Ink in my skin
Blood on a pin
In memory of "your name here"
Time on my hands
this pain I can withstand
for a rose
for a heart
for a tear

Marking this time
Marking my crime
with words etched in blood red and blue
Innocence brings
kisses that sting
like a sad melancholy tattoo

A heart on my sleeve
and a name on my arm
and a highway to hide my disgrace
What I can't bury
I still have to carry
in a hitchhiker knapsack
in a roadside embrace

I pay for my sin
with pain in my skin
and two-hundred dead presidents
I murder my past
and this pain won't last
time buries all evidence

A heart on my sleeve
and a name on my arm
and a highway to hide my disgrace
What I can't bury
I still have to carry
in a hitchhiker knapsack
in a roadside embrace

Ink in my skin
Blood on a pin
In memory of "your name here"
Time on my hands
this pain I can withstand
for a rose,
for a heart
for a tear

THAT'S WHAT THE WHISKEY IS FOR

by Tom Prosada-Rao

You're chasing your past like a moth to a flame
She's not coming back, and nothing's the same
She dreamed herself right out your door
And that's what the whiskey's for

That's what the whiskey's for
That's what the whiskey's for
When you don't want to know anymore
That's what the whiskey's for

Love's such a cruel, a cruel invention
And you played the fool's last shot at redemption
What you can't have – you want even more
And that's what the whiskey's for

That's what the whiskey's for
That's what the whiskey's for
When you don't want to know anymore
That's what the whiskey's for

So the whole world has tipped off its center
There goes the girl, return to sender
When you're the same old slob that you were before

Well that's what the whiskey's for

That's what the whiskey's for
That's what the whiskey's for
When you don't want to know anymore
That's what the whiskey's for

"Front Page" by Laura Hemenway

CUL-DE-SAC

by Cate Graves, Bob Rea & Ben Rea

Slam the door on the Ford Escape
Screeching tires and slamming brakes
Light a smoke to stop the shakes
Halfway gone and halfway back
Serious as a heart attack
Three a.m. in the cul-de-sac
Again

That one night when he moved me in
I was living at my sister's then
Welcome was wearing thin
That was years ago
That was years ago

I remember that first time well
Both those kids were raising hell
Had to break away a spell
Oh the shame I felt
Shame I felt

Slam the door on the Ford Escape
Screeching tires and slamming brakes
Light a smoke to stop the shakes
Halfway gone and halfway back

Serious as a heart attack
Three a.m. in the cul-de-sac
Again

That one time when he got a raise
Put an offer on a bigger place
Ten percent's a lot to save
But anyway
But anyway

I know damn well that I ain't leaving
But it's too soon to go back in
It's too late for looking back
At the way things might have been

Slam the door on the Ford Escape
Screeching tires and slamming brakes
Light a smoke to stop the shakes
Halfway gone and halfway back
Serious as a heart attack
Three a.m. in the cul-de-sac
Again

FOUR WALLS AND
A MURPHY BED

by Dennis Russell

Four walls and a Murphy bed
Lumpy pillow to lay my head
Hot plate and a coffee pot
Everything I need I got

Gideon's Bible that I stole
From the hotel I was at before
Pad of paper and a ball point pen
Everything I need I get

I was a poet 'til the words run dry
If the words don't flow then the bottle's dry
Cry in the bottle when there ain't no wine
Everything that's empty I can go and buy

A draw-chain bulb and venetian blind
Only way to get any light
A night owl's only halfway worldly wise
Everything I see is through bloodshot eyes

I had a job but it gnawed inside
I told the boss to fuck off and die
Ain't got no job, but that work is fine

Everything I earn is everything I find

Plastic bottles and an empty quart
Keeps me from livin' in a cardboard fort
A shopping cart and aluminum can
Everything I work is the B-plan

Dumb luck and acquired skill
Good looks don't pay the bills
Save it all as long as you can
Everything I know I am

The king of the road died a long time ago
I'd take his place, but I don't know
Seems like a big responsibility
Everything about my time now is free

Four walls and a murphy bed
Lumpy pillow to lay my head
Hot plate and a coffee pot
Everything I need I got

THE NIGHT I MET
GEORGE JONES

by Marty Axelrod

The night I met George Jones
He was getting gasoline
Looking anywhere but at me
As I took his credit card

The first thing that I thought
Was he shouldn't be behind a wheel
And on top of that, how bad I'd feel
To be a witness on the news

The night I met George Jones
I didn't get his autograph
Cause he bore down so hard
He tore that slip in half

Then he fumbled with the hose
Spilled some on his fancy boots
Let out a good loud 'God damn you'
I know it wasn't aimed at me

I said 'God bless you'
For every note you've ever sung
He finally met my eye

Gave a crooked smile
And then he hit the road

I should've called someone
To drive him home
The night I met George Jones

I wish I'd called someone
To get him home
The night I met George Jones.

"Untitled" by Laura Hemenway

GASOLINE & LIQUOR

by Natalie D-Napoleon & Brett Leigh Dicks

I've been driving this road so long, I don't know when to stop.
I've been running away so long, always wanting one more
    drop.
I've been holding this bottle so long, I hear your name in every
    song.
Oo-oo-oo, Oo-oo-oo, Oo-oo-oo-oo, Oo-oo-oo-oo.

Gasoline and liquor,
One came on fast, the other acted slow,
Liquor and gasoline,
One made me stay, the other helped you go.

I've been sleeping alone so long, still reach out every night to
    feel your place,
I've been in this desert so long, I know every constellation's
    name,
I've been pumping gas so long so long, I see your face in every
    car.
Oo-oo-oo, Oo-oo-oo, Oo-oo-oo-oo, Oo-oo-oo-oo.

Gasoline and liquor
One helped me lie, the other's fool proof.
Liquor and gasoline,
One broke my heart, the other told the truth.

Heard you're out in Riverside, with a new guy and our oldest
    kid.
I look at the locket of hair in my wallet, ask God forgiveness
    for what I did.
Pour my whisky down the sink, pray it washes away my sin.
Oo-oo-oo, Oo-oo-oo, Oo-oo-oo-oo, Oo-oo-oo-oo.

Gasoline and liquor.
One came on fast, the other acted slow.
Liquor and gasoline.
One made me stay, the other helped you go.

TROUBLE IN A BOTTLE

by Britta Lee Shain

Dancin' at the jukebox, lookin' so proud
Knowin' all the right words, but singin' too loud
Whiskey voice
Lips like a model
That there is trouble in a bottle

Look-y there, how she's shakin' those hips
She's got the whole bar at her fingertips
Smoky eyes
Comin' on full throttle
That there is trouble in a bottle

Don't walk my way, I've got a gun in my car
I'll shoot myself if you come closer
Not gonna get mixed up with you,
I've come too far
My final answer is "Nooooo, sir ..."

Painted on jeans, poured into that sweater
Those red high heels don't make me feel any better
Hair flows like brandy
Kind o' girl I could coddle
That there is trouble in a bottle

Bartender pour me another one
Don't let her be like the other ones
Me and her can have some fun …
Till the hurt hits the fan

You walk my way, I catch my breath
What's sure to follow is sudden death
I'm drunk on love
There's no time to dawdle
That there is trouble in a bottle
That *there* is trouble in a bottle!

THE PARTY GOES ON

by James Houlahan

She holds herself back in the sunlight
but she spends all her cash when it rains
I want to tell her
I do the same

The evening is filled with her laughter
the evening is filled with her smile
I'm feeling better
after awhile

Who am I to wander through this celebration row?
Who am I to riddle all the pain that I know
in a song?
And the party goes on.

I'm looking for a writer to show me
I'm leaning on the authors of old
for some kind of answer
some way home

She's standing at the edge of a doorway
a stack of books they lie at her feet
she does not need them
she is complete

Who am I to wander through this celebration row?
Who am I to riddle all the pain that I know
in a song?
And the party goes on.

It's later now the mob is unwinding
but the music seems to keep it in stride
and she is floating
but on the inside

The night is making good on its promise
to give her everything that she needs
just for awhile
the hunger it feeds

Who am I to wander through this celebration row?
Who am I to riddle all the pain that I know
in a song?
And the party goes on.

Down The Rabbit Hole

with DJ Palladino

by Silver Webb

DJ Palladino is a former newspaper writer and editor who now co-owns with his spouse Diane Arnold, The Mesa Bookstore, a tiny emporium of mostly great books in Santa Barbara. He is also the author of two books, *Nothing That Is Ours* and *Werewolf, Texas.*

Silver: Mesa Books is, in all fairness, a hobbit-sized store. There are women in Montecito with larger closets. And yet, the books you sell are invariably really good ones, as if you have somehow persuaded people to only bring by boxes of the very best used books. Obviously, you read. A lot. How do you curate and maintain such an intriguing collection of books, and has it surprised you that people have responded as well as they have? Every time I come in here, there is someone browsing.

DJ: Well, I'm not the only curator. I push for the things that I like, but there are three other people, the most important of whom is Diane, my wife, who is great with children's books. I know thrillers, but literary stuff, and poetry are my thing. My personal taste is constantly being mitigated by what sells in the store. We recently put a sign on the store that says "Just bring us your best books."

The short answer is, I love to look at books and pick beautiful books. Signed first editions are cool, but I'd rather have a beautiful edition of a book I've never seen before. I'm not shocked people have responded so well, but the place already had good faith, good press, it's been here for 25 years. There was initially some skepticism when we bought it, people who had been shopping there for 18 years, but for any customers we lost, we gained a bunch of new customers. I love the young people who come in from City College and ask "Was this James Joyce guy really any good?" So I spend some time as a used-book mentor.

Silver: Perhaps it's just writers, but most people I know miss having a bookstore on every corner of town, the feel and smell of books, being able to pick them up and flip through them before you take one home. You can divide people into two camps, those who are perfectly happy with a kindle, and those who have strong opinions on soft cover vs. hardcover. Do you think bookstores will make a comeback? Is that why you bought Mesa Books?

DJ: I think they already have made a comeback. Amazon wiped out the big chains, but little used bookstores were thriving during Covid. I don't expect there will be a resurgence of chains though. We bought the bookstore on a whim. Don't let anyone tell you anything different. I had lunch with Nick Welsh from the *Independent* and he said, "It's for sale, you should buy it." It's an open secret, my wife had just retired and she was driving me crazy. She's wonderful, but for years I was used to having all this time to write at home. And I thought, *Oh, I can get her into the bookstore, she'll leave me alone in the morning.* And she thought, *Oh, he'll go down to the bookstore in the mornings and leave me alone.* In a few days, we confessed what we were thinking, and we still bought the bookstore. Within six months of that lunch, we had the bookstore. Now I tell her, "It's my bookstore, leave me alone!" We love it.

Silver: What did the road to writer look like for you? And who are some of your book heroes?

DJ: I'm old! So I feel like I have one more book in me. I'm writing something now, and maybe I'm wrong, but I'm 70 and it takes me a long time to write a book. I plug away at it every day. I really value this idea of having an obsession that unifies your writing. James Joyce is my great writer hero, and that is a promise to work the craft as best as you're capable of doing. The idea of sitting down and writing every day, I love it more and more. When I was a journalist, I loved when it was over. Now I just love doing it, writing fiction. The idea of following the road to wherever it leads, Writers like Flaubert, who have a weird group of stories like *Madame Bauvery* and *St. Julian the Hospitaller,* and just followed the craft of his work. As a journalist, I wrote Sunday, Monday, Tuesday, and the rest of the week I was relieved I didn't have to write. Now, I'm happy to write every day. I always wanted to write fiction, but I never had an idea stick until was about 50, when I started in earnest on fiction.

Silver: Previously you had a news beat at the *Independent,* and it seems you know just about everyone in this town. Did your background as a journalist inspire your mystery novel, *Nothing That Is Ours*, which I believe is set in Santa Barbara?

DJ: Santa Barbara 1958/59. I didn't intend it at first. The inspiration for it, the working title was Castle Rock, because when I was very young, I read about Castle Rock,which was this thing nobody knows about. There used to be a four-story rock and people came from all over and had picnics on it. I couldn't believe that nobody knew about it. Supposedly it was partially destroyed by the earthquake in 1925, and then they used that as a pretext to destroy it, and popular mythology is they used those rocks for the harbor, but it's not true. They built the harbor with other rocks. There was a fight over the harbor. Some people wanted to dredge out the bird refuge and make that the harbor, but people argued for 50 years, and then this guy, Fleischmann, had a big boat and he paid for the harbor, well, half of it. He was the yeast guy, Fleischmann's yeast. And he only paid for it if they put it right there, so they had to get rid of Castle Rock, which changed the drift of sand forever. All kinds of crazy things happened because of it. West Beach didn't exist then. So it was an ecological nightmare, which couldn't have taken place when I was a teenager, but it could take place in 1925. So I started to write a book about that, and I ended up writing a book that took place in 1958. It was like a noir novel, but a lot about Castle Rock ended up in it. Mostly it's about 1959, one of those cruxes in history, things before then were different than what came after, the environmental movement came along.

It was an interesting time to write about. Aldous Huxley came to Santa Barbara in 1959, gave a series of lectures called "The Human Situation" at UCSB that were ten years ahead of their time, all about anti-war, anti-pollution, and LSD. This was so popular that they set out speakers outside the classroom and people from Santa Barbara went up to listen to him talk. I was on the history beat at the *Independent,* so I had a lot of research already done for the book.

Silver: What inspired *Werewolf, Texas,* your latest novel? I know it's set in Texas, but have you seen any werewolves in Santa Barbara?

DJ: I'm a werewolf in Santa Barbara! No, this is so random, as the kids say. I love werewolves, the idea of them, movies about them, like *Werewolf in London*, the original Werewolf movie, all of that. I love the idea of them. They're the Id Monster, they come from within. You transform, but you go back. It's also interesting the combining of human and animal, the idea of metamorphosis, change. There's a mystification when I start writing. I was in Austin, and we were walking down the street, and kept noticing that all these stores had five-point stars in the window, and I thought it would be cool if they were really signs to keep werewolves away. And then I couldn't leave it alone, the novel came out. That's all you need to write, some sort of idea that you can safely obsess over. The things you already have inside of you collect around it, somehow.

Silver: What is the universal appeal of creatures that sulk about under the full moon? Part of the pathos of the original Wolfman, was the fact that he didn't want to turn into a werewolf, and he was tortured by his own nature.

DJ: I don't want to give away too much. One of the games of the novel is to figure out which character the werewolf is. It's not clear who it is. One of the werewolves has gone through everything, has lost everything, and is in love, but he knows he can't be with that person. The torment is there, but there's another side to it, a releasing of the Id Monster. The violence of werewolves is pretty senseless compared to other monsters. They don't even eat their prey, they just kill them. Vampires suck blood, zombies eat brains, but werewolves are pure hatred and anger. It's not pure in a good way; I don't want people to turn into werewolves. I had a young woman tell me once she wanted to turn into a vampire. I said, "Oh, honey, you don't want to do that. You have to kill people." Death is certainly a subject of my book, and what is the price a werewolf pays for immortality? They're cast out, can't live a normal life. And there's a lot of violence. Can you de-fang a werewolf? There's a lot of vampires in books these days where the vampire chooses to drink goat blood. A vegan vampire? I never heard of a vegan werewolf, except maybe the ones in *Twilight,* or maybe they only killed people off stage.

Monsters become metaphors. Vampires, for instance, are a metaphor for druggies. I don't know about Dracula; I think he's a metaphor for foreigners. You don't want to hang around with a Romanian, they're weird!

Silver: As you may have noted, there is a genre of book that dips into the romantic lives of werewolves. Pulp fiction for the furry, as it were. Are your werewolves smoldering beasts of fury and the love that dare not speak its name, or are they regular people, who occasionally need to go out on the town when the moon is full?

DJ: When I finished the book, my wife said, "There's too much sex in this book." Then the publisher read it and said, "There's not enough sex in this book." I didn't know there were werewolf romance novels until after I published it. There's a significant romance in the book, but whenever I write about love affairs there has to be something unexpected. There are many star-crossed lovers in it.

My characters who are werewolves don't remember what has happened after they turn into werewolves, but there's something that persists in their consciousness. When they're werewolves, they don't think, but there are rules about who you can attack when you're a wolf. You can't attack your own child, your mistress, etc.

Silver: As a writer of witches and vampires, I've been counseled by very good writers of literary fiction that subtlety is best, that you have to treat your supernatural characters with the same premeditation and restraint you would show if you were writing *David Copperfield* (let it be noted, Dickens was anything but restrained with his word count). How did you approach writing your werewolves?

DJ: It's magickal realism. You do it because you want to use the fantastic for some reason, to make it interesting or explore something. But you have to adhere to something realistic, certain limitations you want to obey. Part of its believability. You want people to buy into it, so you can't just make them ridiculous, you have to put in limits of reality. Most writers make rules for themselves and their characters, and it happens as you're writing, you decide what they would and wouldn't know. It's a weird pragmatic thing. You know that Disney had this thing called "believable unbelievability." When a character runs off the cliff and they run eighteen steps into the air before they fall? Those eighteen steps wouldn't really happen, but then gravity takes over.

Silver: Do you have any literary plans afoot now? Any events at the bookstore we should be looking forward to?

DJ: I'm working on another version of a novel I started when I was thirty, a mystery involving comedians. And another book set in Santa Barbara, but I'm calling it something else, fictionalizing it this time. There's a witch in it! For the bookstore, I host Sunday afternoon readings, outside, where everyone can join us. We'll have an anniversary event in spring with readings, music, etc. Follow us on Facebook.

Silver: Thanks so much for keeping Mesa Books around and all that you contribute to our community. And thanks for being interviewed.

WEREWOLF, TEXAS
PROLOGUE

by DJ Palladino

Once upon a time I was married to a ghost. We took the vows in throes of passion knowing full well the asymmetries involved. After all, I was fervent earth and up for anything while she was molecular air, antimatter maybe, structured around sorrowful memories. I was a poor ragged man and she came from the invulnerabilising power of money, and loads of it.

But we were lost to love. The hasty wedding happened in a magic moment but you had to wonder what future we were heading for. My daddy's mud barn or her father's mansion? Cohabitation presented problems with one foot on the ground and the other in aether's swirly realm. She thought:

Love will triumph over sense and sensibilities like it always does. I thought: It's all wait and see. Let our kids sort things out. Though what such creatures might look like was wildest conjecture. Coarse, but touched by unexpected grace, for a while I was actually changed. Not by an angel, mind you, but by breathless revenant love.

But one day, the haunting turned into a haunt. Tell you what: She's just spoiled, and that's all there is to it. Father distant as the moon above, mother stewed on the stuff the whole time she was growing up. In the beginning she was fun, though, God. You could tell she was wanting it despite all the internal damages. Thought the best thing would be some kind of take her and then take her hard and that was right on. She opened like a tangerine, booyah, first shed the covers then all fall into moist sections. Sad but that didn't last any longer'n it takes an Austin singer-songwriter like me to mention his truck. Spirit and flesh was how our marriage went awry, I guess. Particularly those last few months, what with her gliding through the house no louder than a soft moan, eyes wistful, remembering, recriminating, no appetite, and so vague you could almost see through her. See through everything she does. Used to come right up behind and ask what I was doing. Made me jump and then get madder, all the time madder at her, the ghostly wife.

***

And on another day, my little ghost just disappeared for a few days, like spooky girls do. I took her on a bit when she came back, I feel bad 'bout that.

But she changed, not me. My lovely little phantom said, "I can't do this anymore."

I said, "Please come back to the sugar shack." And she said no.

Then she said, "What about this? I'll pay rent, but I want my stuff to stay at our old place and me with it in the bedrooms upstairs, you in the kitchen and dining room below till you find something better."

Matter of time, I thought, before this moody soul wants to reintegrate.

Then I overheard her on the telephone, speaking to some other someone, a presence unknown. She said: "Meet me in the park, like back in the day."

***

And now here I am in said park mad looking for my little lost ghost. Mad to sad, turning into one of my own done him wrong songs, slinking down past the jammed-in tendrils trimmed to the edge of this dying place: poisonous oleander or tender evergreen shoots. They grow so lethal and sweet over there. Here we have edibles everywhere: cleaver, hackberry, neglecta, pawpaw, and spatterdock. Lady's Thumb. Also reckon yucca, otherwise known as Spanish Dagger plant, a succulent, sensibly adapted to desert, though bizarre to behold.

Creeping up this row of hedges planted by settlers who fled. Maybe I should flee too, you know? I mean to say: if my ghost is out here, are others? And carnivores abounding in this here frontier between settlements. The salmon evening turned Zane Grey. Maybe bears. Beware. Meanwhile, write a song about it; watch the full moon rim's silver hues about to rise above the desert's dim blues. A bad song.

**

But a big sound. Dark despite the artificial light. She's somewhere near. With her boyfriend maybe whilst her husband, me, is starting to bitch, belch, and complain. His feet hurt in his pinchy boots, his pinche boots. I hear crunching on the pathway.

Then: "Baby?" Her ghost voice rises.

Not summoning me, it turns out, calling him. It. Patient, attentive, it's skulking the low country too; learning to herd me. Guarding and guiding from the lighter places on the evening trail into blue shadows, to end it in darkness.

"Baby? I answer. Didn't recognize my own shaky voice.

Ran into strangers who were not amused. Gunshot you missed me. I slow down looking, but I was looking for my baby, I said. I broke out into the Moon Tower clearing and heard soft padding come from behind. In the dark below the fake moon.

"Show yourself!" I said, the once tough guy sweating in the shadow of the tower.

Then the thing glides out into the clearing too. Exhale through its black nose. Its face ringed with fur and walking like a lowdown thing, growling and sniffing the warm summer air beneath the tower with its own moon above it. I mean I heard what the government said, a plague of these things. But I didn't believe it. They was just trying to curtail my lifestyle.

"What the fuck," says me the blue-jean bro in his off-white wifebeater in the warm evening.

"What the fuck is that," and, like I was in some archaic danse, I bow and square off with the shadow in the changing shadows. On jelly legs, the pit of my stomach roils. I'm burning beer and whiskey now, the smell of the booze ascends over desert perfumes, flowers of abandonment, in the brush beyond the dinosaurs. Nice boy, nice doggie. Circle and dip. Allemande left. Charge and cut off. Growling low now.

"There's nowhere to run," says me out loud looking frantic around and suddenly I throw up.

"Nowhere to hide," I think she answers from somewhere ghostly near. "There there."

The moon in all its phases, she told me, strictly cyclical yet it always felt like a chance encounter. Regularly wax and wane over the tilted planet, as we go crazy about our business. Never knowing when; come out your evening class or your Sixth Street tavern and there it was in a different part of the sky, in a phase you never expected. Yellow like old teeth or flashlight white, auraed in the sky with haze. Stillborn. Complete beauty, though note terror of solitude and a life haunted by terrible dreams.

Alone, brush tangling in my boots, I fall and jump up,

pure willpower, but overwhelmed at once and advantageous it passes. And nicks me. Rushes my blood.

Time to gasp then it passes to slice me again, deeper. Almost surgical. The sharp push, pull, and cut scared to shit when it hit. Sobbing for air as I stand up and realize my Achilles tendon is cut. Stumble down and there is blood. The next hit drove up the old adrenaline to superhuman. I leap up and even with my right foot flapping manage to run and run hard, blood run down everywhere.

Heard someone screaming and realized it was myself. How many am I? In a lit grove is she nearby watching? Is God watching? How many of His Persons are?

And then silence. The moon shone down, no clouds anymore. A rush forward toward where the tower towered. Artificial moon. I hit it hard as the creature hit a chain link fence. Pulled myself up steel rungs. Wolf can't climb, I thought. Something howled, long and expectant.

One day there will be a ballad about the beast below, I thought. Chester Burnett. Dogs begin to bark, hounds begin to howl. I saw the distant remnant lights of Austin. Wait a second: There aren't any wolves out here: Even I knew that. Bears, mountain lions, maybe.

I rip off my t-shirt to make a tourniquet and at about the same time the terrible pain arrives. My blood all over the girders. Reeking of Beam and beer back, I pull myself up farther into the naked iron branches of the tower, and the moon sails far from the clouds once lined with silver, the world and the blood below actually pools. Another howl and I shiver in the warm evening air.

I'll huff and I'll puff and I'll.

Below a soft crunch.

"Baby?" I say, surprised at my own quavering pitch.

I look down and can see nothing but a wind maybe moving the sage around disturbing the air with incense known to cowboys and rattlesnakes. "Baby," I whisper.

Then the thing is on my arms, teeth sunk in so deep and the flesh torn along sliding lines, blood sluicing into the mouth that brought itself back up. Release and reattach, then it tore. As I look down in eyebulging shock my arms mangled to the bone, shreds of tissue hung from coatwire. The visible man. How the human anatomy appears cut in layers to one of my deeper selves. The thing was crawling up the wall, a lover passing over his beloved's body at the neck and tearing me down on the ground tear away my face why my face and eyes without a face and went from fear into a pained paralysis and then the spasm of my body's last drives for survival trying some mad jerk away that only made matters worse and the fear turned into the horror and that turned into the darkness of weak belief and then just black.

Was the last thought I ever had as a man. For an absurd moment beneath the pain looking up at the moon I wondered if eternity would be always colored by this last despair, sagged-out dreams throwing me into an endless room reserved for those deathborn to regret. But more likely, it was just nothing and it would be nothing, the kind we can't even consider, more unfathomable than God's inactivity, an everyday nothing that nullified the entire universe and all of time and us. And all of us. Nothing, not even a ghost left behind. Tell you what, though, we will always think there's more to the goddamned story. Has to be.

WEREWOLF, TEXAS
CHAPTER 3

by DJ Palladino

"Okay, Lila, as you might have surmised, we gotta go," said the tallest cop who bared his head and doffed his cap towards Shaney's date. Polite. But his voice allowed no scintilla of accommodation.

"Now, see here," Shaney said, hearing the hollow, stilted bravado of his own voice. "You can't just march up to a table and arrest somebody like that. Even in Texas."

This remark drew surprised looks from the lawbringing trio.

"What are you saying about my state?" asked the roundest one, more puzzled than offended. "Was that some kind of disparagement, slur, impugnage, whatever?"

Surprisingly, Lila joined the balding cop. "Yeah, John. What does that even mean?"

"I simply meant that you can't just barge in and order us around. It's not the old west. Mr. Dillon, Mr. Dillon," he said, flapping his arms around doing a decent Chester imitation. Shaney might have been a little buttered at this point.

"Who mentioned arrest?" asked the first constable. "And was that a Gunsmoke reference? I watched that show once. The whole set—Dodge City, right?—feels like a retirement home hallucination."

"And yet it was the longest running television program in history, until The Simpsons," said the youngest lawman. "Which must mean something."

"I'm still not sure what he's implying," said the tall gun. "Can I see your I.D., sir?"

Just as Shaney reached for his license, remembering there were 28 hits of his homemade hallucinogens zipped in the wallet, the officer's radio blew its nose. The cop held his hand out to abey John's proffered wallet, and, relieved, John abeyed.

A kazoo voice uttered phrases from the microphone receiver.

"Okay, okay, ten-four, and then we snore. She's coming in," the cop said, annoyed.

"And then we roar," corrected the round cop. "Lila, sil vous plait?"

Shaney's "girlfriend" rose looking nonetheless like it was a lark.

"What about me?" Shaney said, happy to put away the drugs. His date was now officially in interruptus. "I mean, what are the charges against this woman?"

They laughed at him again. Lila gave a little helpless wave as she swept out and off with the officers. "See you soon, boyfriend," she said.

"Bummer," said the busboy at his shoulder. All the help seemed suddenly cooler to the touch after Lila May exited pursued by cops. It wasn't anything actually tangible, but the mood of the room transmogrified. Shaney picked up the check and left a tiny tip for the waitress named Minnie Jo who signed with hearts dotting her I's.

Outside, the full moon was lost behind cloud cover sailing; Shaney thought he saw Louis Lamel stumble by. "Hey roomie," he said. Walleyed, his roommate rolled past.

Shaney stared.

"Whoa," said a busboy outside smoking through his break. "You see a ghost or something?"

Shaney explained nothing in discombobulated fashion. He mentioned the drummer's death and the cops taking his date though. Somewhere a cat hissed.

"The wolf is back," said the young man moving out of shadows.

"What're you talking about?" Shaney said.

"It's the full moon and we haven't had one of these unexplained murders since, well, last full moon. You ask any Austinian."

"I will, indeed," Shaney said, thought about Lila and watched the clouds. Down the street he could see Louis rooted to a corner. The sky was moon-brightening, peekaboo.

"There's this legend," the busboy said, "about the Wuff-man livin' in Austin. Awoowuff. Every time somebody gets killed so the police are baffled, it's blamed on the wuffperson."

"They even blamed it on a thing happened at my house," Shaney said, happy for a concrete distraction.

"What thing?" asked the busboy grinding out his cigarette in a fountain of sparks.

"Our roommate Laurel disappeared. By a lycanthrope was her demise." Said Shaney trying to sound like Yoda.

"Dude, werewolf in your crib? No wonder they took Lila away from you," said the busboy pulling out another smoke.

"What do you know?" asked Shaney, then straightened out. "Hey, I've got to go get my girl, um, my friend, man. Gotta save Lila May."

"Don't worry, man. Lila May is always safe, 'specially with the cops," said the bouncer. The sky's light was broadening. The busboy shrugged and went back in the bar. Shaney asked Mr. Clean where the police station was and got a little growl for an answer.

Meanwhile, not too far away, Lila May was entertaining a cadre of cops sitting not four blocks from the place from whence Shaney embarked as hero.

"You hear about the guy with five penises?" Lila May said at the cop shop, staring directly into the eye of the sole policewoman in the group. She sat on a desktop shapely leg crossed over shapely leg.

"Do tell," said icy-voiced Lieutenant Mary Peapes.

"This guy with five penises goes into a doctor and the doctor says, 'My God you have five penises. That's amazing, I've never seen anything like it,' says the doctor. 'How do your pants fit?' says the doctor. 'Like a glove, says the guy.'"

"He had five penises," said the woman slowly drawling. "That's why a glove."

Meanwhile, outside, John Shaney is stopping people on the street to find out where the precinct station just might be.

He was lost even though the neighborhood was a grid. Panic, slow growing, had changed his physiological functions—raised them to the animal level; sounds, flashing lights, and scents were concatenating as he strode through the mix of urban businesses and old houses. Once in a while a yard would explode into dog howls and inhaled snarls and it pushed his body, his already beating heart and heaving lungs, into overdrive. His search was not systematic and his thoughts kept exploding into pissy rhetorical protests. How could the police do this? Wasn't this America?

Meanwhile.

"Okay one more," Lila said. The police gal moaned. "This woman takes her dog to a vet for a checkup and after a clean bill of health asks the vet what was up with the dog's hairy ears. If you don't like it, says the vet, I recommend a depilatory. What's that? You can get it over the counter in any drugstore, says the clerk. Just ask. So she goes to the pharmacy asks for it. A hair remover, the druggist says. You want Nair. He gives her a bottle and tells her some of the precautions. If you use it on your legs, don't sunbathe for a couple of days. On your underarms, don't use strong soap. But I need it for my Schnauzer, the woman says. Then don't ride your bike for about a week."

The policewoman covers her eyes and pretends to cry. Everybody else is wolf howling with laughter. Schnauzer the policeman screams. One of the detectives arrived to drive Lila home, a courtesy.

Shaney found the building seconds after they left. It had no obvious markings, the better to harbor the fascists, Shaney said out loud. Achtung. Entering, he found an empty lobby with an old telephone on an end table between two shabby couches of an early 1970s vintage—plastic passing itself off as Corinthian. Radar red.

He picked up the phone. "Night dispatch," said the voice on the line.

"Hi," he said.

"Can I help you please," said voice without body, obviously practicing patience.

"I'm looking for a woman, um, name of Lila May, who was brought in tonight."

"Yes?" said the woman flattened into a blue uniform.

"Um, falsely, I believe," he said.

"Listen, I don't care much about your beliefs, please. Was this Miss Lila May arrested? I have no record of any Miss May, arrested or brought in here."

"Shit, I'm sorry. Her last name was Wulfhardt."

"Oh," said the woman. "Why didn't you say so?"

The door buzzed and it took him a second to realize it had been unlocked for him. He caught it just in time. The hall loomed long. The hall loomed empty.

A door opened and a blue-capped head poked out. "Down here," it said noncommittally. "You all just step right in, please."

The policeman looked puzzled when Shaney came through the door into the unhealthy light, bulbs that seemed to buzz with cancer-causing carcinogens. "Where's your friend?" said the cop.

"Excuse me?"

"The guy that was with you in the hall."

"Nobody else. Just me myself and nobody else," Shaney said.

"Nonsense," he said. Then the brittle-chinned cop poked his head out the door. "I could've sworn..."

"Please," said perplexed and vexed John Shaney. "I need to see Lila May."

"Are you her cousin, uncle, brother?"

"No, not... I was with her when she was arrested and I'm here to straighten things out. You see I was with her all evening and she was never in any, she didn't do anything. That is, she was arrested for nothing, which I can testify."

"Arrested," said the officer returning to a crowded desk. "Why was Lila May arrested?" He picked up a phone and barked questions. He grunted an agreement and groaned as one would at a bad joke.

"Just like I thought," he said coming back into the room. "Now you're sure nobody was with you? Anyway, she's not arrested. We just made sure she went back to Wulfhardt. Her ride came."

"She's not here."

"She went home."

"You didn't arrest her."

"Now why on God's Green Earth would we arrest Lila May?"

"You keep asking that like you know her."

"Who doesn't?" asked the officer, now patently annoyed.

"Can you tell me where she lives?"

"Okay, now I'm pissed. Look we have a possible murder at a nightclub. We have the usual Saturday night in downtown Austin. And now I have a guy trying to bilk the police for a rich girl's home address. I fuckin' let you in, but now I wish I had not."

"She's my girlfriend," Shaney said, though his heart was not behind the phrase. Shaney was confused. Why did he say they took her back to Wulfhardt? Wasn't that her last name? "I better go look for her," he said mostly to himself.

"Don't leave mad, buddy," said the other cop.

"Yeah, calm down and go," added a voice from behind a computer, been there the whole time, a voice he hadn't noticed till this second.

He wandered the streets in a kind of sawtooth diagonal, unthinkingly heading for home. The buildings in this neighborhood seemed to alternate between houses of faith and places of low intoxication and assignation. Pick up redemption parlors. To be fair, he too was on a pick up date, and wondering about his cosmic destiny at the same time, well, most of the time.

John Shaney decided then and there his date wouldn't be over till he knew his "girlfriend" was safe. Arriving ahead of himself—he almost didn't notice he was in front of his own home till he saw his car in the street—he entered with the heavy Schlage key hoping someone would be up chatting in the dining room. Someone to set him straight about Lila May, who he had concluded, was known to everyone. Nobody home, darkness and dark ghosts swirling, so upstairs he fired up the old laptop.

Of course, he found her right away on Facebook, but of course, the information was superficially offered, like a gnomic poem without scholarly notes decoding. Friending her now would be a little awkward. Besides, her boyfriending him had superseded it. He would be her rescuer, not her buddy. Fuck it, he would rescue. That was not a decision so much as a wave of whatness. Contact he wanted. Her page said she liked Boethius and Harry Potter. In the bar, she admitted to liking Ovid and Kafka, both Metamorphosi. She was currently obsessed with Kinks songs, in particular the one about people swarming like flies around Waterloo Underground.

He shook his head and Googled "Wulfhardt."

Aha.

A town and a family. Which was named for which? That remained mysterious. What was clear, though: Lila May was the daughter of a very rich Texas oil, cattle, and drug manufacturing lord of the land, respected and feared by plain folk living in the namesake town (well, that much might be conjecture). In fact, she was, they were Wulfhardts from Wulfhardt, a town less than an hour's drive from Austin up into the hilly lands. He went back to her page. Her face, younger yet beckoning him into the future. He decided to find Lila, then and there, Amen. There was even a street address for her papa's home in, of all places, an online phonebook. They had a landline. He packed up the laptop and thought he could be there before midnight, or well before. He would sing outside her window, baying at the moon.

The old green Hybrid ran great, but had suffered from the specific brand of neglect that student economies engender. Everything was nearby, so he rarely drove. Thus, with no gas, oil low, windows dirty, and tires, well… more on that later. But he turned it over and she started right up. Shaney had glanced at a Google map then printed step-by-step directions to take him from his rickety front porch to the porticoed, antebellum columns of Wulfhardt manse in the city of Wulfhardt. He whispered goodbye to absent roomies, didn't leave a note. Last second, he chose a shortcut route through mountains knowing it might end up a winding one lane road. Getting stuck behind some rube in a rusty tractor at this hour seemed unlikely. It was not quite ten as he threw the car from P to D and headed toward the onramp moving all wayward hearts west with headlights lit gold and silver. But something came tumbling after.

In the evening's course of concert and bar Shaney had five drinks but felt no ill effects, he told himself. As precaution, though, he stopped for coffee with refuel at a poison-yellow-lighted highway minimart, and choked down the bitter brew with only Cremora and sugar to dull its grating edge. Tank full and hopped up on the road, Eric Burdon and the Animals singing "Gotta get outta this place" on the radio, he laughed and then tuned out as the radio signal began drifting like a ghost around an FM universe. It sent him eerie half-messages about home security and credit card catastrophes. Gradually caffeine entered his sluice veins and took over.

Shaney saw himself in the dark car window and wondered what the hell he was doing. He was a man of science. Ruled by natural law tamed by logic—the scientific method: you know, theory and proof. His heart was pounding now because he was on a hunt not tempered by reason, but by a supposition too vague to name. The proof was this act, a pudding he could not resist. The vision in the windows was of a mysteriously self-assured night stalker moving with dark grace towards a destiny too murky for even him to understand.

But this reflection on self-reflection lasted less time than station identification on the drifting radio signal, now playing "The Lion Sleeps Tonight," as Shaney, inside his hurtling car twenty-five minutes later headed into scrub-forested hills above Austin city. He saw deer eyes in the bushes; rabbits dared the road ahead of him. He would have no mercy; he was driving hard and being driven to remit his girlfriend's captivity.

The map called it a highway, but it looked like a pitiful stretch of crumbling asphalt with the Harry Potter-ish name Fangtooth Lane posted above bullet-riddled highway signs. Ha, he thought, good thing I don't believe in omens.

He did wish, however, that the night wasn't such a heavy black blank. The road wound up into dark, and the moon was back in clouds. Sometimes glints and reflections below suggested broad rivers or maybe wide lakes lit by streetlamps. It probably was scenic, by daylight. His radio meanwhile had gone crazy. He listened in on a conversation hailing from Nebraska all about the proper use of sheep dip and the horrors of hoof and mouth.

And then like it was right in front of him, Shaney saw the drummer Shug horribly askance with blood flowing from his neck. He shook it off, Pee-tee-ess-in-deed. Then the moon came out, the road reappeared, and Shaney muttered a dark curse. Try not to think of a dead man on a toilet seat.

And by now the asphalt part of the road was losing badly to the dust and rocks beneath it and beneath that sand and sandcrabs stretching to Pacific seas. Probably. Signs were farther and farther apart. The night was buckshot with stars but they seemed distant in this high country by moonlight.

Coming around a long sweeping-to-the-right bend, he

suddenly had to curse and stamp on screaming brakes. There ahead of him in the road stood a zombie. Hair long and furiously unkempt, its face glowed white with an expression of frozen thought: as if its affect had been shut off forever. The manthing began walking towards Shaney in the halting spasmodic way of cinematic terrors evolving from Val Lewton to George Romero. How this horror had stepped out of a movie and into this roadway was the mystery. One answer might be: hallucination.

Waving his hands over his head, "Hey, man," the zombie drawled, "thanks for stopping, dude."

John got out. His car had died in the sudden screeching halt, and he heard a terrible hiss emanating from the front end. What it might mean chilled him far deeper than this apparition with stoner voice.

"Bummer," said the zombie, looking down in the vicinity of tires. "Don't guess you have two spares, man."

He looked at the supposed monster and saw now a shabby man, out late, possibly a stroke victim, in an earlier age, another era, a polio catastrophe.

"Are they both flat? Shit," said Shaney, surprisingly calm.

"Well one is de-eh-finitely fuh-lat," said the lone walker. "Both are as bald as my dead Papa," he laughed. "T'other might leak slow enough for us to limp it over to Uncle John."

Shaney looked at the formerly undead man, uncomprehending, now lost in self-pity and seeing his romantic quest disappear at the sudden onset of bad circumstances.

"What is that, Uncle John?" said Shaney. "A garage? Won't be open this late," he said, despairing sigh in his voice harmonizing with two tires hissing air into the air.

"What. Your… no… your Uncle John's is a kinda cuh-rash pad and puh-arty house right nearby. Somebody there drinkin' nice keg beer and somebody there can fix tires."

"You think," said Shaney, dubious.

"O I know, bra," he said. "Let's hop uh-in and ho-hope fer the best."

They did after changing the left tire quick, motivated by said hope. The drive wasn't far. The zombie gave assurances and the wheels held over the rugged terrain. Shaney had doubts about this guy, especially after smelling him: a gaggy combination of campfire, BO, and sickly sweet alcohol breath. But also something fundamental—so to speak—in his scent. It wasn't death. It was likely unchanged underwear.

"You were scared a me for a second," said lurky man, who gave his name as Junior Lee, like the funk icon robber.

"Seen too many horror films," Shaney said. "Your appearance in the headlights…"

"Thought I was the fuckin' walking deceased," he chuckled low. "Well, you're not too far off. Turn right here," he said pointing to an unlikely opening in the low brush. It was unmarked if it was a road.

He negotiated the turn but everything felt mushy and the car dipped and scraped bumper in a dry culvert across the dirt road. Where are you taking me? John Shaney wondered.

"It's not far, ruh-eally," said the strange fellow now seriously stinking up the coupe. "You know what lupus is?"

Shaney muttered something vague, "A wasting disease." He looked over.

"Yeah. I think I have it. Buh-hummer, huh? You know the name means red wolf? Huh? You know it's not contagious? You know, it's not curable and you know people can't explain why lupus sufferers have it one day and not the next. It comes and goes. What a we know? Most doctors agree that it's a good idea to avoid sunlight if you have it. Hence the zombie lifestyle. You know what exacerbate means?"

"Yeah," he answered. "Sunlight makes it worse. But what difference does it make, if you don't know for sure if you have it?" It's an age of hypochondria, Shaney thought. We live with too much information, and nary enough wisdom.

"What does it all fuckin' mean? Oh, fu-huck, almost missed it, turn here. Avoid the sunlight. It means I'm turning into a monster, fuckin' Duh-racula."

"More like a werewolf, I'd say," muttered Shaney too busy avoiding a boulder to be tactful or sympathetic. His wise-ass American boy self took over.

"That supposed to be fuh-huckin' funny?" asked Lee.

"No man. I'm sorry."

"You are? Pu-ull in here."

Easy for you to say, he thought.

"Wipe that grin off your fuh-face," said Gangster Lee, AKA Junior.

"What the fuck are you talking about? What fuckin' road?"

"Don't mind the stuttering. It's the lupus talking, and don't worry, you're on the road."

"I don't know a lot about the disease, but I don't think it affects language patterns. It's not, um…" Shaney said, trying to think of the name of the disease that made people curse and such. A syndrome. His mind threw up a block. Meanwhile he was stopping in a spot designated by Lee's shaky finger. As he got out of the car, a small gaggle of shadows swarmed out from a dark, bushy area, the shadows exclaimed salutations and introductions entailed as spooks became bodily. Many motley mountaineers here had animal surnames; Rooster, Weasel, and even a Duck.

"Anyway you're wrong," said Lee into his face as they crossed the darkling plain towards a bonfire.

"Actually, I really don't think lupus affects speech, though your walking, well…"

"What's wrong with the way I walk?"

"Don't be so sure, man," said one earnest thronger leaning forward while handing beers and joints, a loaves and fishes thing, as they neared a roaring fire by a dark home. "Diseases have a life of their own, doctors don't know a lot. In the 1950s and 1960s they had theyself a lot of ulcers, blamed it on the rat race. Come to find out it was a virus and not a national malaise, y'all. Stress ain't disappeared but hardly nobody gets ulcers nowadays. Then they was this Yuppie disease where everybody was enervated and tired like all the time. Again, they blamed it on the culture. Just went away like ulcers. About five years ago all my friends started having panic attacks. Didn't even know what the word was but they's so dizzy they'd haveta pull off the freeway. Makes you wonder huh? Everybody's depressed right now. Some day they gonna find out it was a virus, you betcha. I betcha WWI and WWII were virus attacks. People go crazy kill each other. You ever hear tell of the sad virus, my good old friend?"

"Can't say's I have," said Shaney now drawn into the bosom of some boozy fellowship.

"And he's a scientist," said Lee, though Shaney couldn't remember telling him anything such like.

"Okay, Doctor Science, listen to this. About a year ago, I got a flu going around. It was a weird one, I admit. Didn't have those classic syndromes or symptoms, and the fever came on so slowly, I didn't even know I was hot till some girl told me."

"You give me fee-vah," said one of the clan between slurps from a jar, going all Peggy Lee on it.

"Anyways, I succumb to this malady and my friends took care of me. But once in a while I found myself alone in their house. And when I was I would think about things and sometimes stumble across some bad memory or dismal meditation, you know."

"Like you do," said someone.

"As you must," said someone else.

"And then I just started bawling. I mean crying my eyes out, great blubbering, nose-draining lamentations."

"Lachrymosity," said a gaunt man leaning against the house Shaney saw in the black surroundings, in the dark surrounding the heat blaze.

"So anyways, I get better, back on my feet and I get back in the race only to run into some goodtime buddy in a crosstown bar and he says, where y'all been. I told him I was sick, some weird flu. And he says me too. He was a little drunk you could tell. And he sidles up to me and says, 'The damndest thing. Every time my old lady left the house I started cryin' like a baby.' Three days later, five friends told me the same thing."

"You talk to a doctor?" Shaney asked. Everybody laughed.

"Must be a college boy. One what has that, whatayoucall in-surance stuff we read about up here," he drawled accent on the "in."

"Think about it, though. My emotional life controlled by a microscopic parasite. I was transformed from the he-man you see before you into a baby girl bitch wailing for her mommy. The implications are staggering."

"Vis-à-vis identity and fuh-ate alone," said Gangster Lee.

"Vis-à-vis," said the man on the house, echolalic, "fate."

"Hey," said one of the good old boys, who were mostly in their early thirties, "speaking of priests."

"Here we go," said another.

"How do you get a nun pregnant?

This caused considerable head scratching and finally Lee said, "I give up, Dogboy."

"You fuck her," he said, accent on the verb.

Howls of laughter and knees slapped, but in the midst of it, Shaney heard a low, long lamentation. Someone is always crying, he thought.

Then the longest and scariest wolf keen he ever heard outside a horror movie rolled across the horizon and rang in valleys filled with dark night, causing a deep silence among the roisterers.

"She's out there tonight," said someone.

She? Thought Shaney.

"So what is it you want here, partner?" said the lanky man by the house directly talking to John, who was still wondering who "she" was.

Then he realized he was being addressed. "Oh, me," he said.

"Oh my," someone else said.

"I got a flat back on the road and ran into Mr. Lee here," said Shaney as a chorus of Mr. Lee, Mr. Lee, Ooh Mr. Lee broke out behind him.

"You cannot fix a flat?" asked the gaunt man with an unmistakable tone of disapproval, contempt actually.

"Two flats," said Lee, chiming in. "One spare. By the way, Uncle John, this man is a professor from the University, a man of science."

"Why did you not say so in the first place?" said Uncle John moving with catlike grace down from the porch and face to face with Shaney. "An intellectual. An academia nut." The man had a long face ending in a pointed beard, not quite Mephistophelian but more sinister than a Carradine brother.

His face caught shadows and gave off deep secret vice and easily offendable honor.

"I'm just a grad student," said Shaney. "A research fellowship that hasn't actually begun. Next quarter next," he stammered. He was frankly unnerved by Uncle John's animal magnet field.

"Where you headed tonight, doc?" asked the bass voice host.

"I'm uh-off to Wuh-wulfhart."

"He talks like you, Gangster," he said. "Hope it isn't catching. What's goin' on in Wulfhardt, uh duh-hoctor?"

Shaney looked up, recovering. "If you can't fix the tire, I understand. I was just doing what our mutual friend here suggested. I'm sorry for intruding."

Uncle John considered the man in the firelight, the light that danced on the windows of the house and on the wire-rimmed spectacles of the onlookers and dully in the glass of the beer bottles in every hand. "Don't be like that," he said. "We're glad to help you, partner. I just forget myself bein' up here amongst the jackalopes and ky-oats."

"Now you're makin' fun of us, boss," said Gangster Lee.

Uncle John snorted. "Here friend, have a beer and maybe a toke of this good hill country dope while I look at the damages."

Shaney tried to ward off the proffered joint, but people weren't hearing it. The stuff tasted kind of funny and as he headed towards the car with Uncle John, he felt an enormous load leave his spirit. Here at last, he thought, all prayers to the mute and deaf heaven will actually be answered before articulation. John turned to him and said, "I'll take a look, don't bother yourself none. Head over to the fire and get acquainted. But I might need the key."

Reluctantly, Shaney dug out the chain on which his whole life hung. New home, the lab he had barely been allowed to touch at school, his storage bin back home, containing all the ingredients for the psychedelic party fuel, of which fruit, he suddenly remembered he was holding. Uncle John bopped off with a young woman in tow, he hadn't seen her previously, the rest of the crowd being decidedly male. Uncle John said, "No worries," over his shoulder.

At first, the conversation around the fire was promising. People began telling stories about their own long trudges through academia, with an overwhelming tone of wistfulness. "What are you all doing now?" asked Shaney, genuinely interested.

After an awkward silence, one of the more thoughtful-looking amongst the throng said, "Well, my friend, you know, I was an economics and communications double major and after a brief but exciting internship at the state capitol in beautiful Austin, I'm expecting to be a made barista at the Brown Water Fusion Emporium just down from the shadow of the legislative house. Sometimes I see my old boss. Motherfucker."

"Enough about us, perffessor. We never did hear what yer business in Wulfhardt might be so urgent on a Saturday night or is it Sunday morning?" drawled one particularly red-eyed firemate.

"I'm looking for a woman," he said. "The police dragged her off and I'm trying to figure out what happened," he answered, though surrounded by good old boys grilling him, he knew it sounded hollow.

"I had a woman once," said someone across the flames after reflection time passed.

"What's her name and occupation, doc? Maybe we know her."

"Lila May," Shaney said.

That sent ripples of laughter and nudges through the group. "Next thing you'll tell us, it's Lila May Wulfhardt, since you's gointa Wulfhardt and all," said another amidst renewed peals of laughter.

He looked at the group and said nothing.

"Oh, shit," said one of them. "It is her, iddunit?"

"Oh fuck," said another. "Why diddun you say so right away?" He went off calling Uncle John. As he left the fire another long howl rolled across the hills and vales. The group suddenly seemed sober.

"You know her a long time?" asked one of them silently.

"Just met her. Actually she's in my section. I'm her TA."

They looked at him as if he spoke a foreign language.

Uncle John returned. The woman with him looked concerned. "Why didn't you tell me?" he asked.

"How would I know, whatever," Shaney said.

"Come with me," he said and led Shaney into the brightly lit house. "Hungry? Help yourself," he said. There were slabs of beef brisket and mountains of ribs heaped on a table pooled with meat juice, blood. Beans bubbled nearby. Uncle John pulled out another joint (drugs not meat) and made a big deal out of lighting it as if the wind was beating against him. He handed it to Shaney. "Why didn't you tell me?"

"I'm not fucking sure what it is I didn't tell you now."

"Lila May was arrested?"

"Oh, yeah."

"You saw them read her her rights?"

"Well, not exactly."

"What did the pigs say?"

"Some bullshit about making sure she went home."

"Good, that's good. Tell me now, don't make me guess. Was she at the concert where that guy died, the drummer?"

"Soleil cou coupe," said the woman, reading from a book in the living room.

"Wow word travels fast. Yes, she was. With me. I'm John," he said thrusting out his hand to the woman. She grasped it weakly and then turned it over to observe his palm.

"Non," she said. She looked at John.

"Well that's a relief. You protecting her and all. I'm gonna go out on a limb and say she knew the drummer."

"I guess yes. How did you know?"

"I'm gonna fix your car and I'm gonna suggest you go home. I mean home to where your parents live. Somewhere safe. Meanwhile take a toke of this. And a beer. By the way, usually people bring something when they come to a party."

"I wasn't prepared. Didn't know I was coming."

He looked unconvinced. "Think. I bet you have something to share, maybe wisdom."

"Wait a second, there is something." He realized he could kill many birds with one stone and took the psychedelics out of his wallet. "There's about 30 hits there," he said.

"Fuckin' A," said Uncle John. "You did bring something. See?"

Pretty soon the crowd was crowding around feasting on the little blotter hits, some took two or three. Shaney didn't care much. For one, he was beginning to feel the effects of whatever it was that was in Uncle John's joint. (He doubted it was pot.) Besides, there were sheets of the stuff back in his room and binders full of it in his storage space back home. He had made the batch of molecular-altered hallucinogen a year ago with his student loan money. It cost him in the low five figures. He had profited like a pig from that batch and now was quite happy to give back to the community that had made him fat.

The drug was fast-acting. Unlike regular stuff that took half an hour of insinuating change, his formula, nicknamed Waterbear, came on like a rocket with spectacular special effects but less of the mystical. You got high without considering the omphalos of the universe in everything, and usually got happy too. Some people creeped; not often.

Soon the place was roiling in pleasure's grip. Uncle John, who had delayed his gratification, smiled ear to ear over the salubrious mood that had overtaken his midnight barbecue. He had come in after 15 minutes working on the tire and washed his hands, free of grease but not of his many sins. He liked the idea of transcendental fun: from wake and bake to nodding out. He took Shaney by the arm.

"Now they will be ready for anything, including the end," he said.

Shaney, a little fuzzy about the implication, or maybe whether or not it was a quotation, a book or a movie, pointed at an iron bent into the shape of Texas hanging by the door, maybe it was a triangle to call the diners forth and hence.

"What is it with you guys down here," he said hiccupping. (No dope ever had made him hiccup before.)

"What what?" said the bearded host Shaney, idly spitting toward the fire. "What guys down where?"

"Texans. The state you live in is some sort of talisman to you. You know, or maybe you don't, most people in America save their patriotic fervors for their hometown if anything. Yay, Brooklyn, Frisco, whatever. Californians, who have every right to consider their state as a kind of paradise show no similar—hic—obsessive possession by location, bilocations—hic—the boundaries, the morphology of some artificial delineation brought about by rivers and political motivation mostly. To make an arbitrary shape into an icon you'd hang on your garage door. It's as if it were a crucifix posted to let others know why you are the way you are. I'm a Texan, it says, and it doesn't matter if you're a hipster—hic, hic—from Austin or a hick, a hick from the mud country up near Louisiana, you are the

Texan—the proudest child of the second biggest state."

"Are you through?" asked Uncle John. He made a sign with hands flat, one roofing over the other at right angles.

"Time—hic—out?" said Shaney.

"T is for motherfuckin' Texas," said the host. They crossed the small pasture land and neared Shaney's car. "Aww, goddamn," said the deep-voiced Texan. "My girl said it would be done but where the hell is she?"

"Looks done," said John feeling ready to launch.

Just then some clouds cleared above a long line of trees and the full moon shone down on the land. Shaney thought it was a Universal Pictures kind of moon and remembered the long, low howl of that which his newfound friends referred to as a "she." On cue, the thing rolled out its most baleful wail yet, sounding much, much closer now.

"A coyote, right?" said Shaney noticing that Uncle John's steps had become a little stumbly, if that's the word he wanted.

"Motherfuckin' wolf," he said. "Where's the girl?" he asked, though the question sounded almost rhetorical. "Let's head back. We must've missed her going up the other way." He took a long look at the car and reversed his steps.

Shaney looked around and, even though it was dark then, bright now with a moon that cast shadows, it seemed pretty clear there was no other way that they would have failed to see the young woman charged with changing his tires. "Hey, man," he said. "Looks like she's almost done. I'll just take it from here. I got to get on the road."

"What's your hurry?" said Uncle John. "You got it bad for her?"

For a split second, Shaney thought he meant the wolf. "Lila," he said, realizing. "She's my girlfriend," he added, chuckling.

"Really?" said John. "Really. How nice for you."

They had reached the fire where, by now, the whole pack was engaged staring into the flame in throes of ganglionic ecstasy.

"Heard the wolf, anyone?" said John sarcastically. "Seen the girl?"

"Chupacabra," said one of the more diligently transfixed coterie.

"O, don't get started on that, again," said somebody.

"No shit," said John. "It's just some misplaced angst about illegal aliens."

"Chupacabra was here first. The wolf came from up north."

"What is it?" asked Shaney.

"Mexican werewolf."

"Except there's no were there," said the cohort's owl-eyed grad student barista dreamily. "The chupacabra was never human. Besides it eats only goats."

"Then Unkie John is fucked. The goatman saith hey, where is the fucking girl?"

"Okay, all of you. You know where I stand on this issue. Draw pentagrams, drink a beer, or go away, fuck you, I stopped caring. As for you," he said to Shaney, "come over here." He motioned impatiently toward the house. "I can't blame you for getting everybody so high. It was my idea. Downright generous of you," he said, though his tone seemed to deny his gratitude. He rummaged through an end-table drawer and suddenly grunted. "Here," he said holding out yet another tiny pin joint wrapped in yellow paper. "Have a hit of this before you go, it'll protect you on the road."

"What is it, wolfbane? I think I've had enough drugs and medieval lore for one night."

"You fuckin' kiddin' me?" said Uncle John, who seemed to get larger and gruffer as he spoke. "The wolfman isn't from the Middle Ages. No. The wolfman was invented in Hollywood. Sure there was lycanthropy since Freud and before I guess, but all of the stupid warning signs and vulnerabilities—silver bullets and shit—were invented by a coupla screenwriters."

"All the more reason to…" The howl came again.

"Yeah. All the more reason to fear the thing in and of itself. It's cinema, and that means bigger than life. Only God is bigger than life, amigo. And he most decidedly does not exist. Smoke it and I'll honk your horn in five minutes or so. Oh, and give these dogs here some idea when they're coming down and what vitamins to take afterwards. I might need'em after all."

He trudged off to the house and pulled out a rifle, the moon well past the rags of cloud coursing high. There was a box of kitchen matches. John Shaney decided to light it, take one hit and throw the rest in the fire. Turned out one was more than enough.

"I think it was the wrong joint," was what he was trying to say from the back door to the happiest campers by the firepit. How it came out was, "I'm mink in the Hmong void."

This amused the crowd, though nobody noticed Shaney had had trouble opening a screen door, so he ripped through its scrim and stumbled across the short clearing between the stoop and the bonfire as if the walked-upon earth had suddenly become a tipping ship. When they did stop laughing at his unintentionally absurd declaration, they still found themselves amused by his attempted careen to the car, which ended far short in soft bushes.

Shaney lay down now over compressed baby tumbleweeds. (Excellent eating, by the way.) He had some desperate thought about how his trip down to Wulfhardt had not gone exactly as it was half-assed planned. He concluded the conscious moments of the waking hours constituting his "day" with a fascinated survey of some dirt inhabited by night-walking ants. He thought they probably did not sting. He thought about hope and hopelessness; will and surrender, He signed off with that thought merrily ringing in his ears, they don't bite. Then a distinct usurpation of the local laughter by horrible shrieks he sort of heard coming from the fireside.

The [Un]Usual Suspects

Marty Axelrod

Marty performed as Party at My Cave, the Zoom concert series, throughout the pandemic lockdown and beyond. Marty is a founding member of the singer-songwriter collective Tall Men Group. As a keyboardist and drummer, Marty does recording sessions and live gigs to accompany a host of talented artists. Marty produced and co-wrote (with Nicole Gordon) the beloved concept album *Songs of Shiloh*. His songs have appeared in numerous TV and movie soundtracks. Link to "The Night I Met George Jones": partyatmycave.bandcamp.com/track/the-night-i-met-george-jones.

Lori Anaya

Lori Anaya, presenter, and bilingual elementary school teacher in Ventura County for 36 years. She's published in short story and poetry. A number of middle-grade projects and picture book manuscripts are currently in review. Active member of the Society of Children's Book Writers and Illustrators. She commutes daily to Ojai to visit her horse, Ruby.

Heather Bartos

Heather is a writer living outside of Portland, Oregon. Their personal essays have appeared in *Fatal Flaw, Stoneboat Literary Journal, miniskirt magazine,* and elsewhere. Their flash fiction has appeared in T*he Dillydoun Review, The Closed Eye Open, Tangled Locks Journal,* and elsewhere, and their flash piece "Goldfish" won first place in the 2022 *Baltimore Review* MicroLit Contest (will be published soon).

James-Paul Brown

Santa Barbara based artist James-Paul Brown, blends the broad brushwork and vibrant colors of Van Gogh with the ethereal strokes and pastel shades of Monet to produce enchanting, passionate masterpieces. A world-renowned painter his life resembles a colorful palette, capturing the beauty and adventure of the human experience. His broad range of subjects include Hollywood celebrities, famed athletes, and world leaders, as well as favorite cities, landscapes and vineyards.

Admired by art-appreciators around the world, his works continue to be discovered. His love for sports has resulted in paintings and sculptures for the 1984 and 1996 Olympics, the Las Vegas International Marathon and the International Swimming Hall of Fame. In the late 80s, he was chosen to capture the courageous beauty of the Americas Cup.

Mary Elizabeth Birnbaum

Mary Elizabeth was born, raised, and educated in New York City. She has studied poetry at the Joiner Institute in UMass, Boston. Mary's translation of the Haitian poet Felix Morisseau-Leroy has been published in *The Massachusetts Review,* the anthology *Into English* (Graywolf Press), and in *And There Will Be Singing, An Anthology of International Writing* by *The Massachusetts Review,* 2019 as well. Her work is forthcoming or has recently appeared in *Lake Effect, J-Journal, Spoon River Poetry Review, Soundings East,* and *Barrow Street.*

Gary Carter

Gary's poetry and short fiction have appeared recently in *Nashville Review, Sky Island Journal, Deep South Magazine, Steel Toe Review, Dead Mule, The Voices Project, Silver Birch, Live Nude Poems, Delta Poetry Review, Real South Magazine* and soon in *Main Street Rag*. Based in North Carolina, he also produces non-fiction for print and online pubs, and sells a little real estate on the side.

Christopher Chambers

Christopher is an editor, bartender, and teaches in a prison. He's the author of three books: *Delta 88* and *Kind of Blue* (fiction), and *Inter/views* (poetry). He is past editor of *Black Warrior Review, New Orleans Review,* and *Midwest Review.* He's been spending a lot of time lately in Milwaukee. www.christopherchambers.net

Ted Chiles

Ted came to creative writing after moving to California in 2003. With a Ph.D. in Economics, he taught Economics at the undergraduate and graduate levels. In 2013, he completed an MFA in fiction from Spalding University. Chiles' fiction has been published in print and online and consists of short stories and flash fiction. Originally from the Rust Belt, Chiles lives in Santa Barbara with a writer and two cats.

Beth Copeland

Beth is the author of *Selfie with Cherry* (Glass Lyre Press, 2022); *Blue Honey*, 2017 Dogfish Head Poetry Prize winner; *Transcendental Telemarketer* (BlazeVOX, 2012); and *Traveling through Glass,* 1999 Bright Hill Press Poetry Book Award winner. Her poems have been published in literary magazines and anthologies and featured on international poetry websites. She was profiled as poet of the week on the PBS NewsHour website. Beth owns and operates Tiny Cabin, Big Ideas™, a retreat for writers in the Blue Ridge Mountains.

Chella Courington

Chella's prose and poetry have appeared in numerous anthologies and journals including *The Los Angeles Review, lo-ball magazine, Gargoyle, The Tusculum Review, Danse Macabre* and *SmokeLong Quarterly.* In 2016, Courington published *was it more than a kiss* (Flutter Press), a chapbook of poetry. In 2015, she published *Love Letter to Biology 250* (Porkbelly Press), a chapbook of microfiction, and *Flying South* (Kind of Hurricane Press), an e-chapbook of poetry. In 2011 she published *Paper Covers Rock* (Indigo Press), a flipbook of lined poetry; *Girls & Women* (Burning River), a chapbook of prose poetry; and *Talking Did Not Come Easily to Diana* (Musa Publishing), an e-book of linked microfiction. Her latest publication is *Adele And Tom: The Portrait Of A Marriage.* Her work has been honored by *Camroc Press Review, The Collagist, Qarrtsiluni,* and *Main Street Rag,* and nominated for Best of the Net and Best New Poets Anthology.

Natalie Damjanovich-Napoleon (D-Napoleon)

Natalie is an Australian-American writer and singer-songwriter. Her writing has appeared in *Meanjin, The Australian (Review), Entropy,* and *Writer's Digest* (US). She has won the Bruce Dawe National Poetry Prize and has released a #1 Independent music album. Her debut poetry collection *First Blood* was released in 2019. She recently completed her second poetry collection on motherhood in the wake of the Trump presidency. Currently

Natalie is completing a PhD on historic amnesia.

Joe Ducato

Joe's previous publishing credits include *Wild Violet Magazine, Strata Magazine, Avalon Literary Review,* and *Sandy River Review,* among others.

Brett Leigh Dicks

Brett is an American/Australian photographer and writer. His work has been published in newspapers, magazines, and journals ranging from T*he New York Times* to *Griffith Review*. For the past 25 years his photographs have been exhibited in museums and galleries around the world, in both solo and major touring exhibitions. He has co-written one song ... and Doug Pettibone played on it.

Marco Etheridge

Marco is a writer of prose, an occasional playwright, and a part-time poet. He lives and writes in Vienna, Austria. His work has been featured in more than sixty reviews and journals across Canada, Australia, the UK, and the USA. Marco's volume of collected flash fiction, "Broken Luggage," is available worldwide. When he isn't crafting stories, Marco is a contributing editor and layout grunt for a new 'Zine called *Hotch Potch.*

Alexis Rhone Fancher

Alexis Rhone Fancher is published in *Best American Poetry, Rattle, Verse Daily, The American Journal of Poetry,Plume, Diode, Flock,* and elsewhere. She's authored nine poetry collections, most recently, *Junkie Wife* (Moon Tide Press), *The Dead Kid*

Poems (KYSO Flash Press), *Stiletto Killer* (Edizone Italia) and *EROTIC: New & Selected* (NYQ Books). Her photographs are featured worldwide. A multiple Pushcart Prize and Best of the Net nominee, Alexis is poetry editor of *Cultural Daily*. www.alexisrhonefancher.com

Fritz Feltzer

Fritz dropped out of a graduate program three units before achieving a degree that would have allowed him to teach at junior colleges and state universities. He lives in a flatulent RV where he writes narrative poetry on a portable Olivetti typewriter and studiously defaults on his student loan. His most recent chapbook, *Steampunk Ahab*.

Cate Graves

Cate writes little songs…little songs that are raw. Sometimes they are sparse…sometimes filled with lots of little words. Often they are written about things like tasting sweet orange on your lips and wanting to kiss someone so that they might experience tasting sweet orange on their lips. Cate Graves likes kissing. And singing. She hopes you will listen in and sing along. kategravesmusic.wixsite.com/kate-graves-music
"She captures moments of human emotions in beautiful snapshots, vignettes and sighs."—Mary Gauthier
"Cate Graves gives the world her new record of brave, unaffected, fragile lyrics and vocal performances."—Melissa Ferrick

Jen Hajj

Jen follows her muse wherever it takes her: artistic dabbler, folksy songstress or lazy daydreamer. Jen recently moved from Idyllwild, CA to the edge of the Ozark National Forest, where she grows tomatoes, plays banjo on the front porch, and snuggles with her partner, Kurt, and the wee dog.

Laura Hemenway

Laura was Professor of Music at Antelope Valley College in Lancaster, CA, from 1978 to 2009. She was Music Director/ Conductor of the Antelope Valley Symphony from 1978 to 1997, and served as Advisor for Antelope Valley College's Commercial Music Program from 1997 until 2009. Laura "retired" in 2009, and moved back to Santa Barbara, where she has served as Music Director for Out of the Box Theatre, has played cello, piano and celeste, with the Santa Barbara City College Orchestra, and has served on the board for the Goleta Valley Art Association. She is a painter and her work can be seen at https://www.etsy.com/shop/LauraHemenwayArt.Her favorite activity is playing accordion and singing backup on gigs with her husband, singer-songwriter, Dennis Russell.

James Houlahan

James is a singer, songwriter, and guitar player based in Los Angeles, California. He grew up in Concord, Massachusetts, and studied philosophy at the University of Chicago. Houlahan has come to be known as a songsmith who channels both tradition and poetic innovation, rooted in alt-folk sounds and eclectic Americana. His sixth album *Beyond the Borders* will be released in November 2022. Houlahan's songs have been used in commercials, television, and film. For more information, please visit jameshoulahan.com.

Stephen Dean Ingram

Stephen's writing has appeared in *Gulf Stream Magazine, Potato Soup Journal,* and other publications. His fiction and nonfiction focuses on identity and how we place ourselves within this world. He makes stir fries, writes stories and novels, and lives with his wife Mary and Olive the tabby princess in New Mexico.

Maryanne Knight

Maryanne's short stories have been published or are forthcoming in the *Santa Barbara Literary Journal, The Yard: Crime Blog, On the Run,* and *Grand Dame Literary Journal.* Born in Brooklyn and raised in Vermont, she now lives and writes in Southern California. MaryanneKnight.com

Shelly Lowenkopf

Shelly is a writer (short stories, novels, essays, and reviews), editor (books and magazines), and teacher (graduate level, undergraduate, and adult) who lives in Santa Barbara. He has learned from first-hand experience how much more difficult it is to write books that have been sold before they were written than to sell books that have already been finished. For this and other reasons, he has been called an ironist.

Amy McNamara

Amy's poems have appeared in numerous journals and have been nominated for a Pushcart Prize. Her first novel, *Lovely, Dark and Deep,* won an ILA Children's and Young Adults' Book Award, was an ABC New Voices Pick, and was nominated as an ALA Best Book for Young Adults. Her second novel, *A Flicker in the Clarity,* was published in June 2018 from HarperCollins. You can find her at amymcnamara.com and @amynkmcn.

DJ Palladino

DJ is a former newspaper writer and editor who now co-owns with his spouse Diane Arnold, The Mesa Bookstore, a tiny emporium of mostly great books in Santa Barbara, California.

Tom Prasada-Rao

In May of 2020, Tom Prasada-Rao wrote the song of his life, *$20 Bill (for George Floyd).* Peter Blackstock of the *Austin American Statesman* called it "song of the year probably—I mean this is a song Bob Dylan should cover." It has since been covered over 200 times (though not yet by Dylan). "Tom is the most compelling presence to emerge in the singer-songwriter genre as I've seen in a long time" —Jim Bessman, *Billboard*

Ben Rea

Ben grew up in Durango, Colorado, and currently resides in Nashville. His musical influences include Bob Dylan, John Prine, and Jason Isbell. His co-writes have appeared on albums by Bob Rea, Cate Graves, and Jody Mulgrew.

Bob Rea

A Colorado native, Bob Rea now works out of Nashville, Tennessee. He has released four albums and is currently working on his fifth. His latest album "Southbound" has received critical acclaims and includes two songs written with Cate Graves. It reached the number four spot on the Euro-Americana charts. His unique guitar style, compelling lyrics and powerful performances provide an intimate and sometimes humorous glimpse into American life.

Dennis Russell

Santa Barbara-based singer-songwriter Dennis Russell has released 5 albums: *My Little World, Primitive-Acoustic-Sensitive-Singer-Songwriter-Type-Guy, Golden, 7 of Townes,* and *Plain: Primitive-Acoustic-Sensitive-Singer-Songwriter-Type-Guy, Too.* He's opened shows for Cyndi Lauper, Dan Bern, Katy Moffat, Rosie Flores, and Lili Haydn, and moderated songwriting master classes and lectures by Suzanne Vega, Allen Toussaint, The Del McCoury Band, Dan Wheatman, George Kahumoko, Jr., and Irma Thomas. He has also self published a book of short stories, *That Fourth of July,* and a book of poetry, *Surfer Songs.* Dennis continues to write and perform with his wife as The Dennis and Laura Show,, and can usually be found at a club, coffeehouse, or concert venue somewhere on California's

Central Coast. For concert dates and recordings visit www.dennisrussellroad.com or www.reverbnation.com/dennisrussell

Britta Lee Shain

Britta Lee Shain was born with a transistor radio in one hand and a pen in the other. At six, she began playing classical and popular piano. At twenty, a James Taylor concert at West Hollywood's famed Troubadour (with opening act Carole King) inspired her to buy her first guitar. Coming of age in the 60s, she spent pivotal years at UC Berkeley, where her early musical tastes were shaped by Janis Joplin, Joni Mitchell, Leonard Cohen and Bob Dylan. After trying her hand at screenwriting, novel writing, and even writing a memoir about her travels with a rock and roll band, in 2001 she turned her creative energy to songwriting. Britta's acclaimed memoir *Seeing The Real You At Last (Life and Love on the Road with Bob Dylan)* was on the *New York Post's* "40 Best Books of 2016 You Must Read Immediately." www.brittaleeshainbooksandmusic.com

Max Talley

Max is a writer and artist who lives in Southern California. Talley's writing has appeared in *Santa Fe Literary Review, Fiction Southeast, Vol.1 Brooklyn, Atticus Review, Litro,* and *The Saturday Evening Post.* His crime thriller, *Santa Fe Psychosis,* debuted last spring and his short story collection, *My Secret Place,* was published in September by Main Street Rag Books. www.maxdevoetalley.com

Rebecca Troon

Rebecca is a songwriter, singer and musician living in Santa Barbara. A California native, she spent her childhood in Southern Oregon. Rebecca sees songs as passageways for processing life. Gifts she receives that she can then share with others. "It is an honor to be of service through music. One of the best parts is that through recording songs, they can go out in the world on their own, and hopefully be helpful to others, and sometimes I hear about that."

Silver Webb

Silver is the editrix of the *Santa Barbara Literary Journal.* Her food-writing and interviews have appeared in *Food & Home, Still Arts Quarterly,* and *Pacifica Post.* Her poetry has been in *Peregrine* and *Burgeon.* You can find her stories in *Danse Macabre, Underwood, Litro,* and *The Good Life,* as well as in the anthologies *The Tertiary Lodger, Hurricanes & Swan Songs, Delirium Corridor,* and *Running Wild Anthology.*

Steven Werner

Steve's a lot of things. Biker, sailor, adventurer, folksinger, poet, songwriter He lives aboard his sailboat in Ventura Harbor. His songs have been sung and recorded all over the world. Through the years he has shared stages with the likes of Bob Dylan, Willie Nelson, Ramblin' Jack Elliott, Mary McCaslin, Peter Yarrow and many more. His duets with Fur Dixon produced four albums of pure California folk gold.

These days Steve plays shows rarely and, like Nosferatu, only when invited. When not invited, he is perfectly content to sail his boat, ride his motorcycle, party with his friends, and live small.

Borda Books

www.santabarbaraliteraryjournal.com
All titles available on amazon.com.

Made in USA - Crawfordsville, IN
72805_9798362988586
11.29.2022 1302